THE WEEK BEFORE CHRISTMAS

A Christmas Novella

by
Jennifer Rawls

This book is a work of fiction.
Any resemblance to any person, living or dead, is coincidental.

Copyright © 2016 Jennifer Rawls
All rights reserved.

This book is dedicated to Jackson,
the greatest gift of my life,
and to my Mom and Dad
with much love and gratitude for all the wonderful
Christmases.

Countdown: 6 days until Christmas

CHAPTER ONE

Miguel rubbed his hands together vigorously, trying to warm them as he walked briskly down the sidewalk. His gait was stilted by the layers of clothing he wore. He had on a short-sleeved and a long-sleeved t-shirt with a sweater on top. He'd found an old pair of shorts at the bottom of his drawer and put them on under his jeans. Over that, he wore his parka, a knit hat and gloves. Still, the bitter cold and whipping wind made warmth unlikely as he walked the last long blocks home.

He'd been walking and goofing around with a couple of buddies from his homeroom. Walking with guys who made him laugh and joke kept the wind at bay somehow. But Eric and Stephen had dropped off by the bank on the street where they both lived. Miguel covered the last part of the walk home by himself. He wasn't afraid; it never occurred to him that there was anything to fear. But he was cold and getting colder.

He could have ridden the bus with his sisters, but he spent enough time with them already. He needed a little time with just the guys, even if it meant walking home in the freezing cold. At least he'd thought it was a good idea when the last bell rang signaling a welcome break from school and the beginning of the Christmas holiday.

He was almost to the corner where he would turn left and then walk the last three blocks. Before his turn was the entrance to Crandall's Department Store. It was the biggest store he'd ever seen, and it always smelled good inside. But his mother had warned him and his sisters not to go inside. For some 10-year-old boys, it might have been too good to resist. Miguel knew that if his mother warned him, there was good reason. Normally, he passed without a thought, ignoring the ornate window displays that advertised things he could not afford. Even on the rainiest days, he walked right by the huge glass doors as if he was oblivious to the shortcut the store provided.

But today it wasn't raining. Today was freezing cold, more than freezing actually according to the big thermometer on the bank.

He looked to his right and left, making sure that his mother was nowhere in sight. She had an uncanny knack for knowing where he was and what he was doing at the most awkward times. She should still be at work, miles away, but he still looked. And looked again. He shivered once more as the wind blew straight through his clothes and skin, right to his bones. It was one of the easiest decisions he'd ever made.

He pushed open the doors and entered a world he barely knew. He'd been inside the store exactly three times in his life. The first time was to buy shoes for school. The second was to buy a white shirt for church. The last time was when he'd walked through, just like today, on his way home. When his mother found out, she'd told him not to go in unless he was planning on buying something, which they both knew was ridiculous. That particular day had been seventy-two degrees and sunny. He'd been feeling really good until he'd mentioned the shortcut, as he recalled. Surely she would understand on a day like today.

Miguel timidly took a few steps inside the store, already feeling warmer. It was as though he could hear his clothes defrosting on his body. The people who worked and shopped at Crandall's looked like the people he'd seen in movies. They were beautiful and wealthy, buying necklaces and silk ties and fine suits. The shoes his mother bought him at Crandall's were real leather. They were glossy with shine, and the laces were stiff at first. He'd felt like a king when he put them on, and he'd worn them until his toes almost poked through the ends. He knew he didn't belong where the rich people shopped. At least not yet. Someday he would buy all his clothes here and if his mother or sisters needed anything, they would have it. He would work hard and be a famous athlete one day. He'd make millions of dollars. That was his plan anyway.

In the center of Crandall's first floor stood the tallest, widest, biggest Christmas tree he could have ever imagined. He thought it was at least two hundred feet tall and had more than a million lights and decorations. Of course, in reality a 200-foot tree wouldn't stand in the middle of the store's three stories without a hole in the roof, but it wasn't much of an exaggeration to Miguel. He stood in awe for several minutes, taking in all the gold angels and jolly Santa Clauses around the tree. The white lights glittered like stars, and he almost salivated at the boxes underneath wrapped in gold paper with red and white ribbons. It was a great tree, he thought, even if it didn't have any handmade marshmallow decorations or family pictures. He wondered what kind of decorations the other two floors had, but he couldn't take the time to explore.

Just walking inside had been a daring adventure that he would definitely not share with his mother.

He'd meant to walk straight through the store, from front to back, not making eye contact and certainly not stopping to browse. But the tree, the decorations, and exotic scents of the perfumery slowed him down. All the salespeople were nice, smiling at him and asking if they could offer some assistance. Everyone was filled with the holiday spirit.

The shining gold bracelets and rings had him wishing to buy one of the delicate necklaces for his mother. She would wear even the smallest locket with pride, he knew. He stopped, not daring to touch, but looking as closely as he could at the workmanship of the sterling silver pieces. He was so caught up in the intricate, minuscule designs that he didn't notice when a tiny gold necklace caught on the scraggly hem of his worn jacket. It weighed close to nothing, and he never felt it dragging along with him as he weaved toward the store's back entrance.

When the security system bleated in alarm, pinging at him from all directions, he went wide-eyed in surprise. As a security guard came toward him with a menacing frown, Miguel knew his mother had been right. Nothing good could come from taking the shortcut.

CHAPTER TWO

Eugene Winters sat behind the row of monitors and watched the people in his store. His face was fleshy, gravity and microwaved dinners taking a toll after sixty-eight hard years. His eyebrows hung low over small eyes that were mud brown in color. His lips always formed a hard line, even when he attempted to smile which, truth be told, wasn't often. He looked cold because he was a cold man, hard-hearted and hard-headed.

He reached for a large white nondescript porcelain mug of coffee. The hot drink was bitter and black, strong enough to walk out of the generous cup and stride out the door. No telling how long it had been in the pot. It was just the way Eugene liked it. He slurped, taking care that it didn't spill on his spotless dark blue uniform shirt. The shirt, especially the patch that identified him as the Chief of Security for Crandall's, was his sole source of pride. He'd served in this store, the flagship, since he returned from the Vietnam War.

He'd joined the Marine Corps voluntarily at twenty after learning that his father had no intention of letting his son ever do more than simple oil and tire changes in the auto shop. College had held no attraction for Eugene, and he wouldn't have made the cut anyway. He decided not to wait for an involuntary invitation from Uncle Sam. He went in as an unruly, spoiled, smart-mouthed kid with little future and came home a disciplined man who appreciated routine and rules. His dark blue pants were always perfectly pressed with a crease that could cut paper. His shoes were always clean.

He missed the polished military version, but his feet appreciated the practicality of the athletic brand the store provided. His white socks, like the t-shirts he wore every single day under his shirt, were spotless.

He believed he was the ideal security chief. He was smart, cunning and could think like shoplifters or grifters. His store didn't have the security issues that the big boxes did and, even though no one said so aloud, he knew that he was the person standing between the store and the criminals. He didn't need a gun, which was a good thing since Crandall's wouldn't hear of it. He was just as qualified, just as serious and just as successful as he had been forty years before when he walked in the door for the first time.

The only thing he couldn't do was get his boss to take the security detail seriously.

Eugene supervised a crew of six. They were veterans, like him, but much younger. He made sure they appreciated the opportunity they'd been given and that their office was always squared away. He knew they ridiculed him when they thought he was out of earshot. They came in thinking theirs was a cushy job with little to do. He corrected them early and often. If they were looking for a plum job with no responsibilities, they could keep on looking.

He used the bank of monitors in the security office to spy on his own men as much as look for shoplifters or other threats. He read journals about the retail industry and knew that the days leading up to Christmas were a prime time for people with sticky fingers to frequent stores. There would always be cons who were successful at walking out with a five-finger discount, but Eugene wouldn't make it easy for them. Security for Crandall's store and the Crandall family was personal to him.

His mind wandered to his unlikely friendship with the old man, Oliver Crandall. The two first met when the old man's son had been killed in a firefight somewhere along the Dong Nai River. Eugene, newly hired and eager to please, had stopped Mr. Crandall late one afternoon to offer his condolences. Oliver had received countless expressions of sympathy, but something about Eugene's words rang truer than all the others. When he learned that Eugene had returned from the same area where his son lost his life, he wanted to hear all about it. He wanted to know what kind of conditions they lived in, what they did every day. Eugene told him everything he could in his coarse way, holding nothing back in answering every question directly and honestly. In no time, Oliver Crandall had come to count on Eugene almost as a confidant. He was the one person who would be totally and unapologetically honest with the older man. Everyone else told him what they thought he wanted to hear, always trying to please the boss.

Years later, Oliver decided to retire and leave the store to his grandson. He tried to talk Eugene into retiring, too. But Eugene was built for work. He had a routine that involved putting on a pressed uniform every morning, right after calisthenics, and watching the men he supervised and the people he protected. The younger Crandall didn't appreciate his contribution, his honesty, or his routines. Just that morning, he'd brushed off Eugene's suggestion that they beef up security around the jewelry counters to discourage shoplifters.

"Mr. Winters," Jake Crandall had said with a lopsided grin after listening to Eugene's suggestion for less than five minutes, "we have the best monitoring equipment in the business. Every piece of designer jewelry is tagged with a special sensor and our associates are trained to call you when they have the slightest inkling that a customer might pose a threat. That doesn't count the sensors at all the entrances and exits. Hopefully, there will be so many people in the store in the next few days that they can barely move. Your guys will just add to the traffic and make it more difficult for shoppers to navigate the aisles. The one thing we literally cannot afford to do is make it harder to buy."

"Well, I appreciate that Mr. Crandall," Eugene replied, "but I just don't think I'd be doing my job if I didn't make recommendations to improve our security, especially at this time of year. Your grandfather," he tried to remind the younger man.

"Isn't here," Jake interrupted. They eyed each other with something akin to grudging personal respect and a healthy dose of professional skepticism. "I appreciate your concern, Mr. Winters," Jake broke the silence. "I trust you and your crew can keep the store and our guests safe, as always, using the resources we already have in place." Jake reached for a file on his desk, effectively quelling any further discussion and dismissing his security chief. The older man took the hint and left the office without a thank-you or goodbye, keeping his shoulders straight as he walked away.

It was that kind of morning that had him second-guessing his decision about retiring. The store's security was all technology based and futuristic. It had been different in the old days before security tapes and cloud-based backups, whatever that was, and a camera on every cell phone. In the old days, working security was like being a detective. Now, it was more like babysitting computers. And Eugene hated computers.

He took another swig from his mug and had just placed it back on the plain brown cork coaster when the alarms sounded. He was embarrassed when the sound made him jump like a frightened schoolgirl. The alarms sounded so infrequently that he almost didn't recognize it when he heard them. One of his guys immediately called him on the walkie-talkie.

"I've got it, Chief," his man said. "Looks like a kid. I'll bring him up."

"No, I'll meet you there. Hold onto him," Eugene replied. Maybe they couldn't add measures to prevent stealing, but they sure could make an example out of the thieves they caught.

CHAPTER THREE

Jake Crandall was an old man at thirty. He sat at his desk, head in his hands, and wondered where all the years had gone. As a boy, he'd loved coming to the store with his grandfather. Everyone was always nice to him and asked his opinion on everything. He'd loved it.

He just hadn't realized he'd be solely responsible for it. Every day, someone reminded him that his grandfather would have done things differently, better, smarter. He didn't disagree. The old man had retired on what seemed like a whim to Jake. He told himself repeatedly that Oliver would come back. He just needed some rest and relaxation. He'd never been known for taking vacations, and he just needed a break. Or so Jake had thought and prayed.

Oliver had taken to retirement like a fish took to water. For two years, Jake had tried to run the store to Oliver's standards - and he'd felt like a failure every single minute of that time. He knew the store needed updating in so many ways. The dressing rooms were tired. The floors needed replacing. The colors were dated as were the displays. Crandall's was a relic, originally founded by Jake's great-great-grandfather, and he wasn't sure that anything had changed since then except the products they sold. When he'd no longer been able to deny that it was his to run, he'd begun making a list of the improvements he thought needed to be made. As the list grew daily, so did his desperation. Fortunately for the Crandall's, they were the only game in town. Literally. Crandall's Department Store had the unique distinction of being the most successful and longest-standing store in a town of about 40,000. Other businesses had succeeded, of course, but Crandall's was the mainstay. People from all around, mostly smaller towns, shopped there. The whole place was what outsiders would kindly call "charming" when they really meant old, stately, boring.

Jake had studied business in college and done well. Truth be told, he really wanted to make his own mark on the store and its lineage, but he was afraid. Afraid of failing and destroying all his family had built and stood for. Afraid of succeeding and making people forget those who had come before. He'd tried so hard to walk a very thin line between honoring the past and jetting into the future with new ideas and fresh approaches to retail, that he had become completely ineffective.

Jake hated being ineffective.

He spent his time playing "what-if" and planning changes he probably wouldn't make or making sure people knew his success came on the shoulders of the Crandalls who had come before. He forced himself to walk a tightrope between the future and the past and he always felt like he was losing his balance.

Even the store personnel put him in this same bind. Take Eugene Winters, for example, he thought while he poured a cup of coffee from an urn his assistant kept fresh in his office. Eugene had worked directly for Jake's grandfather, and he was one of the few men Oliver had really trusted. Jake could no more fire him than he could fly. But Eugene's methods were overbearing. He'd become somewhat of a laughingstock. Most of their employees overlooked him, others completely ignored him. And all because he took his job very, very seriously. How could he convince the proud, older man that he needed to relax, learn to use new technology and try to relate to the people around him rather than trying to intimidate them? Eugene was the definition of old school in a world where new school was all the rage. He was a by-the-hard-cover guy in a social media world. There had to be a way to help Eugene succeed without patronizing him. Jake just hadn't been able to find it yet.

Jake sighed heavily and ran a hand through his thick, dark hair. Maybe he'd ask his grandfather for advice. Again.

He'd just reached for a file with the latest financial data. Crandall's business was steady. Even during the recession, the holiday shopping season had been good for them. Jake believed they could easily triple their revenue, and pay for much needed upgrades, if he just tried a couple of the ideas he'd been thinking about. Maybe he'd ask his grandfather about those ideas, too, he thought.

As always, Oliver would remind Jake that the store was his now, and he should follow his gut. But his gut, and all other parts of him, were Crandall through and through. He wouldn't, couldn't, risk losing it all after they'd worked so hard to build it up.

He'd just taken a big sip of caffeinated coffee when he heard the alarm trigger. He knew from the specific alarm that someone had tried to leave the store with something they hadn't paid for. Without much concern, he returned to his file. If there was one thing he knew for sure it was that Eugene Winters would deal with the shoplifter. And look forward to the opportunity.

Jake perused the file before him with little attention. He knew these numbers almost by heart. He knew the cost and profitability of every line in the store. He knew what products only sold when they were deeply discounted and which they couldn't keep in stock. He could predict an upswing in cooking at home and when there was a new national sports hero. His store offered a microcosmic view of the economic world in general. Anyone who paid attention to stock and prices would be able to see what he saw. He truly never realized that his ability to see beyond the shelves in his store was how Crandall's continued to succeed. His recall for every single bit of financial data, no matter how small, was a unique talent.

"Stop touching me," he heard from a loud, young voice outside his door. The volume surprised him. But the fact that it sounded child-like stunned him.

He opened the door and found Eugene Winters holding a boy by the collar of his scruffy jacket. The boy's feet barely dragged the ground; his nose was red from the cold. Jake couldn't tell if he was angry or scared. Probably both.

"What's going on?" Jake asked, looking from the boy to the man holding him. The boy continued to squirm, tears forming in his eyes.

"We caught him red-handed, Mr. Crandall," Winters said. The look he gave Jake was almost, but not quite, one of pride. He'd stopped to answer Jake's question. He held Miguel by the shoulder roughly, causing the boy to wince and try to pull away. That only resulted in Eugene clamping his viselike grip on him harder.

"What was he doing?" Jake asked.

"Shoplifting," Winters replied matter-of-factly. He held up a gold chain with a dangling heart. Jake knew the retail price was $19.99, on sale this week for $14.99.

"I didn't steal anything," the boy yelled. Winters rolled his eyes.

"Okay," Jake said, holding out his hands as if he was approaching a strange dog. "Is your mom or dad here in the store?" he asked.

"No," the boy said, harshly rubbing his eyes.

"What's your name?"

"I don't have to tell you that," came the reply. He wasn't being belligerent, or at least Jake didn't think so. His voice was shaking, belying any bravado he tried to muster.

"Why won't you tell me your name?" he asked, coming

closer.

"Because you're a stranger," the boy said honestly. Again, Winters rolled his eyes.

"Don't worry, the police will get his name," Winters said, moving to push the boy toward his office.

"Just wait a minute," Jake said a bit sharply to Eugene. "Where are your parents?"

Winters sighed loudly. He had his man. He knew Jake would go soft, let the boy go with a stern warning and a promise not to steal again. Jake didn't live in the real world where boys stole from their own parents if it suited them. Eugene had seen it in his neighborhood time and time again. The downfall of America's youth began with a small stumble. He'd do his part to put an end to it if Jake would just stay out of his way.

Miguel finally met Jake's eyes with his own. "My mom is at work," he explained. Then another thought seemed to terrify him more than the idea of the police. "Please don't call her. I didn't do anything, I didn't steal anything. Please don't call her," he begged again.

"We have the whole thing on video, Mr. Crandall," Winters said.

"Have you watched it?" Jake asked, astounded that there would have been an opportunity in the few minutes that elapsed between the alarm sounding and Winters arriving with the boy in tow.

"Not yet," Winters admitted. "As soon as the alarm sounded, my team was on it. The kid didn't move. The necklace was hanging out of his pocket." Case closed.

"Do you know how the necklace got in your pocket?" he asked Miguel. Again, this time with exaggeration, Winters rolled his eyes.

"No, but I didn't take it," Miguel said again.

"Look," Jake explained, leaning down to Miguel's eye

level, "I'm kind of in a bind. You're too young to be in the store without supervision. Your parents aren't here, and you don't want me to call your mom. You won't tell me your name, and you did have my necklace in your pocket. I'm not sure what options I have," he explained.

Miguel looked down at his worn shoes. He released a heavy sigh. Finally, decision made, he looked at Jake. "My name is Miguel. I don't want you to call my mother because I'm not supposed to take the shortcut through the store. I wasn't shopping, and I wasn't stealing. I was just going home after school." His nerve was slipping but he continued to fight the tears of frustration and fear that threatened to fall. He was beginning to understand that he wasn't going to just be able to walk out of the store and go home.

Eugene stood behind him, smirking. It was clear he didn't believe one word the boy said. For some reason, Jake wanted to believe the kid. Actually, he did believe him. But as he'd explained, he didn't have many good options. The one thing he knew for sure was that he didn't want to get the police involved so close to Christmas. Not only did it seem like an overreaction, it would be horrible publicity for the store.

"I'll go ahead and call the cops, boss," Eugene said, seeming to read Jake's thoughts and arguing against them.

"The police?" the boy exclaimed. His resignation immediately turned to fear.

"Okay, okay," Jake said, making a calming motion with his hands. "I don't believe we need to involve the police," he said directly to Eugene who couldn't manage to hide his disgust before Jake saw it.

"Thank you, mister," Miguel said. He was hiccupping with his effort to remain composed. His face was turning red, and the tears were falling freely. He'd immediately known he was in trouble when the big mean man brought him upstairs to the offices, but he hadn't understood that the police could have been called.

"Here's what we're going to do," Jake looked from Eugene to Miguel. He was going purely by instinct. This was a situation unlike any he'd faced before. But neither the older man nor the young boy questioned his instructions. "Mr. Winters is going to get my car, and we are going to take you home. We'll talk to your mom about what happened, and then we will decide what to do. Got it?"

Miguel nodded affirmative and wiped his eyes. Eugene tugged his thick gloves on without comment, looking Jake in the eye the entire time. He was trained as a soldier and he would follow orders without question. But it was obvious that he was in full disagreement with his boss.

Jake took his wool overcoat from the closet in his office, pulling his leather gloves from the pocket. After telling his assistant he was leaving for a while, Jake led Miguel out the store's front entrance and into the waiting sedan idling at the curb. Jake opened the back door and gestured for Miguel to get in. Miguel eyed him suspiciously. It hadn't occurred to Jake that the boy would have been warned repeatedly never to get into a car with a stranger. Miguel hesitated.

"Go ahead," Jake directed. "I promise we are just going to take you home."

Miguel crawled into the backseat, followed by Jake. The windows were tinted, the seats were warm, and the heat in the car felt wonderful. Under any other circumstances, Miguel would have probably been asleep in minutes after pushing every button and lever within reach. But he was still scared.

He was scared of the man driving the car. He was scared the cops would be called, and he'd be taken to jail. But most of all, he was scared of what his mother was going to do to him when she found out what happened.

"I need an address," Eugene said gruffly.

Miguel gave him the address with a sigh. He had no

hope whatsoever that they would drop him at the door with a warning and a "Merry Christmas."

Jake hid his surprise at the address that Miguel gave. It was an area he knew well because it was only a couple of streets over from his grandparents' house. The neighborhood boasted homes that had stood for decades. They were among the most elegant and stately houses in the city.

Maybe Eugene was right, Jake thought. Maybe this boy was trying to steal to see if he could get away with it. The worn jacket and shoes could have been a sad attempt at a disguise. Anyone who lived in Miguel's section of town likely had the means to buy a dozen of the necklace in question. Still, Jake wasn't going to jump to conclusions. He felt sure he didn't know the whole story.

They pulled into the driveway of a grand Tudor style home. The elegant stone, stucco and half-timbering architecture with its gabled roof reminded Jake of old English estates he'd seen in history books. The bright red bows hung on every shutter and the huge wreath on the massive front door gave the otherwise ominous house a feeling of welcome and warmth. Jake could imagine sitting by the fire and reading, a glass of port at his side. He mentally laughed at himself. He didn't know why these houses brought out the nineteenth century in him. He rarely just sat and read, and he didn't like port.

"This is your house?" Eugene asked Miguel, not bothering to hide his surprise.

"Yes, at the end of the driveway," Miguel said glumly. He'd been terrified that they would call the police. As he drew closer to his house, he almost wished they had; his mother would be much worse. "You could just let me out here, and I could walk the rest of the way," he made one last-ditched effort.

"We could," Jake said. "But we won't."

Fat, wet snowflakes began to fall as Eugene stopped the car and got out, closing the doors behind them to try to keep as much heat inside as possible. Miguel hung his head and wondered how he had gotten into this position. All he had done was walk through the store to stay warm. His mother had been right to warn him against doing that very thing. Nothing was worse than when his mother was right.

The men walked toward the sidewalk that led to the front porch of the mansion. When Miguel didn't follow them, they turned to him.

"I live here," he said, pointing to a much smaller building. Jake had assumed, correctly, that it was a garage. Or it had once been.

With a cocked eyebrow, he looked at Eugene. Eugene, in turn, shrugged.

Miguel was reaching for the door when it flew open right before his eyes. "Miguel, where have you been?" a young woman asked. "I've been worried sick." She grabbed him in a tight hug, dropping her chin on the top of his head.

The woman pulled back and gave the boy a serious once-over then turned to Jake and Eugene. She had seen the car pull into the driveway and the men get out of it with her son. She didn't recognize either of them. "Who are you?" she asked, instinctively pulling Miguel behind her.

"Hello," Jake stepped forward, extending his hand. "I'm Jake Crandall. I own Crandall's Department Store," he said as if that explained everything. When she didn't respond, he gestured to Eugene. "And this is Eugene Winters, my chief of security."

Eugene stood in front of the luxury sedan. With the headlights illuminated behind him, he looked even bigger and more menacing than normal.

"What can I do for you gentlemen?" the woman asked. Jake stepped back, dropping his hand and trying instead for a charming and hopefully disarming smile.

"We had a little incident at the store this afternoon," he began. He noticed that, even with a furious scowl, she was lovely. Smooth skin that looked as if she'd just been out in the sun which was impossible given the gray sky and falling snow. Her eyes were pools of dark chocolate, and her long, dark hair had been pulled into a tight ponytail. He couldn't have guessed at her age. She definitely looked young. But there was a wisdom and wariness in her eyes that bespoke life experience. One thing was obvious: she wasn't the least bit intimidated by either of them.

She looked Miguel in the eyes and asked, "What happened?" Jake was surprised that she hadn't asked him or Eugene.

"Mama, I know I wasn't supposed to, but it was so cold, and I was late because I forgot my math book and had to go back for it. And it was cold, and the wind was blowing real hard. And I was almost to the corner but I saw Crandall's. And I know I'm not supposed to, but I just wanted to be warm for a minute, and it was so cold. So I took the shortcut and walked through the store. But I didn't touch anything. I promise. I just walked through and when I got to the back door, all the bells and alarms went off. And that man came," he pointed to Eugene, "with a bunch of other big guys and said that I stole a necklace. But I didn't. I promise I didn't. It was just cold. And I know I wasn't supposed to. I'm sorry." It had all come out in a rush, in one breath. When he was through, he hung his head. He knew he was in trouble, but he hadn't shed a tear. He hadn't been defiant, either. He'd just explained as any ten-year-old would.

When Jake heard Miguel's explanation, one that the boy had repeatedly declined to give him, he instinctively knew that Miguel was telling the truth. Eugene wanted to put a child through an inquisition, which was bad enough. But they'd scared the boy to death for no reason whatsoever. And all over a necklace that retailed for less than twenty dollars.

He raked his hands through his hair. Before he could decide how to handle the situation, Miguel's mother looked at him.

"My son didn't steal anything," she said matter-of-factly. He ignored Eugene's "humph" behind him. "I'm sorry he was in your store. He knows better," she said, eyeing Miguel with a look that Jake recognized as the "we'll talk about this later" look.

"Mrs..?" Jake began, stepping slightly forward again. This time he let the question hang in the air.

"Shaw," she finally provided. "Cassie Shaw." Jake offered his hand again and this time she accepted the handshake.

"Mrs. Shaw, I believe you." Eugene cleared his throat loudly and made a production of getting back into the car and starting the engine. Jake glanced back quickly and then returned to their conversation. He was actually glad Eugene was out of earshot.

"My security chief got a little ahead of himself this afternoon. We've been worried about shoplifting during the holiday season and, well, he obviously thought he saw something that didn't happen," Jake said.

Before Cassie could reply, another small head popped out from behind her. "Hi!" the little girl said happily. "Santa's coming soon!" she squealed and ran back inside, having delivered her holiday cheer.

Jake smiled at Cassie who was rolling her eyes and shaking her head from side-to-side. Miguel, sensing a shift in the tension, giggled. Cassie rearranged her features into a serious look again and turned to him, "Go inside, Miguel. Your sister did your chores so you'll do hers tonight. Go ahead and start your homework, and we will talk about this later. I'd appreciate a recommendation on your punishment, too."

He looked forlornly at Jake and gave him a small wave before walking into their house.

"I said I believed him," Jake said again, not understanding why the boy would be punished.

"Yes, so do I," Cassie responded, crossing her arms in front of her. "But he's not supposed to take the shortcut through your store. None of this would have happened if he hadn't."

"Okay, I understand," Jake said, although he didn't. The boy had been cold. What could it have possibly hurt for him to walk through the store?

Cassie couldn't have cared less whether Jake Crandall understood her reasons for punishing Miguel or not. Her son was hers and hers alone. She'd been raising her children without anyone's help or permission for a long time. Still, she appreciated the fact that he had brought Miguel home safely and had kept Eugene in check. If he hadn't, things could have gotten a lot worse and a lot more complicated.

"Thank you for bringing him home," she said. "I appreciate it. I hope you have a happy holiday."

"It was no trouble. Merry Christmas to your family, too," Jake smiled. For some reason, he wanted to stay right there and talk to her all night. It was totally unlike him. He didn't get personal with anyone. He was good at greeting and helping people find things and then moving on. He didn't stand in doorways in the snow and make small talk. And he certainly didn't make small talk with married women who had two children.

He gave her a last smile and nod and then turned to the car. He sat in the front passenger seat. Eugene had already the car so that it faced the street, and he was pulling into light traffic before Jake's seatbelt was fastened.

CHAPTER FOUR

Neither Jake nor Eugene said a word on the drive back to the store. Jake was going over every detail he could remember about Cassie Shaw. Eugene stewed over his work being so easily dismissed. How was he supposed to keep the store safe if his boss was going to let every thief they caught off the hook?

When it became obvious that Jake was going to let Miguel go without so much as a warning, Winters sat in the car and watched as Jake talked with the boy's mother. He'd seen the little girl peek around her mother's legs. He knew Jake was intrigued with the family's situation and thinking about what he should do next. That was Jake's problem. He was always thinking, never doing.

Winters had a rare opportunity to show Jake what he should have done without being obstinate. He would go back to the store, pull the video and prove that the kid was trying to steal the necklace. Once he had irrefutable proof, Jake would realize he needed to listen to Winters more often. He'd used a similar tactic with young officers in the Army. It usually got him where he wanted to be without embarrassing his superiors.

He dropped Jake off in front of the store, parked the car in the back lot and then went directly to his computer in the security office. Two of his guys were there, goofing off as usual on their cell phones. When he walked in, they suddenly remembered they needed to patrol the store. Alone, he worked the keyboard and pulled up the afternoon's video from the jewelry counter.

He fast-forwarded until the rolling clock on the screen indicated the time he thought Miguel would have walked through the store and stopped to look at the necklaces. Within seconds, he saw him in living color, wrapped up in his layers of clothing. Just as he had described, the boy made his way through the store, careful not to touch anything. He stopped for a few seconds, a minute at the outset, to look at the glittering jewelry. The necklace in question was on a display table behind him with hundreds of others. As he moved away from the counter, the tag got caught on his jacket. He walked away with no idea the necklace was there. He couldn't have planned it. As Miguel had pleaded, it was nothing more than an accident.

Winters watched the video two more times irrationally hoping that something would change. He wasn't a man who always had to be right but he hated being wrong. He had accused a boy, a ten year-old, of stealing. If Jake had done as Eugene suggested and called the police, they would have immediately asked to see the video. He would have been mortified. He'd put them all through a great deal of trouble because he had jumped to an awful conclusion.

He should have watched the video before going to Jake. He should have listened to Miguel. He'd had plenty of chances to get this right. He'd been determined to prove a point to Jake, to the guys who worked for him and to himself. He'd messed up. Big time.

As a good and loyal soldier, he knew what he had to do. He had to take responsibility.

Jake was going over the employee schedule for the next few days when Eugene knocked on his door.

"Mr. Winters?" Jake looked up from his paperwork. He had hoped to avoid any more confrontations with the man at least for the remainder of the day.

"I know you're busy, Mr. Crandall, but I need to talk with you."

"Okay," Jake exhaled, hoping to relieve some of the building tension. "What's up?"

Eugene didn't sit. He stood in front of Jake's desk, ramrod straight with arms at his side. Jake could never admit how intimidated he was when Winters stood before him like that. Instead, he reached for his cup of coffee, sat back and crossed his legs casually, trying to remind them both that he was the man in charge.

"Sir, I owe you an apology," Eugene began. "As soon as we got back to the store, I watched the video from this afternoon." There was no reason to further identify the video. "The boy, Miguel, was telling the truth."

Jake didn't say anything for a long minute. He rubbed his forehead with one hand and thought about what his security chief said. He was having trouble getting past the admission that an apology was due.

Eugene was uncomfortable with the silence. He was used to a swift and loud response. He was afraid Jake was going to fire him. Where would he go? What would he do?

Jake had been trying to find a way to let this man go for months. He now had a reason, a good one. But he just couldn't do it. Instead, he wanted to find a way to help him. "Please sit, Mr. Winters," he pointed to one of the guest chairs on the other side of his desk.

Eugene did as he was asked, certain he was about to be fired.

"It takes a strong man to admit when he's wrong and to take responsibility for his actions," Jake began. "I think I know you well enough to know that you have already thought of one hundred different things you could have done differently today."

"Yes, sir."

"I'm also certain that you did not mean to cause anyone, including Miguel, any harm. You were just following your instincts and training."

"It seems, sir, that your instincts are much more reliable than mine," Eugene looked at him.

"Please. Stop calling me 'sir,'" Jake smiled. "Coffee?"

"No, thank you."

"Mr. Winters, you have good instincts, reliable instincts. You have been a loyal employee for decades and I hope you will be here until you decide it's time to move on." Jake saw the older man's eye twitch, an involuntary sign of relief. Jake realized then that Eugene was terrified of losing his job. He'd taken responsibility anyway. That action alone spoke volumes about why his grandfather admired the man.

"I owe you an apology, too," Jake said.

Eugene looked at him questioningly.

"I haven't given you the kind of support you need. I know you need more computer training, for instance. You have done nothing but make every effort to keep my family and my store safe. I just assume you're going to be here, doing what you do, day after day. We will do better."

"Um, thank you," Winters responded uncertainly.

"Let's get through the Christmas rush and then you and I are going to sit down together and talk security from the top of the store down to the basement." Jake stood, energized by his decision and needing to get back to work.

"That sounds fine, sir," Eugene answered as he stood. Before he walked out of Jake's office, he offered his hand. Jake returned the firm handshake with a smile. He hoped Winters had been humbled but not humiliated.

They would start over soon and they would both be better for it.

Countdown:
5 days until Christmas

CHAPTER FIVE

Jake couldn't get her off his mind. He'd thought about their brief conversation, run it over in his mind a hundred times, since the previous night. He had no idea what it was about her - the quiet strength and obvious determination, the fierceness of her belief in her child or the hint of financial need - but something tugged at him and hadn't been willing to let go.

During his weekly conference call with his buyers, his daily meeting with the accountants and his walk through the store to greet his employees and customers, he found himself looking for Miguel. He knew the boy would never take the shortcut again. Probably not on a dare or a bet. It was also the first day of the local schools' holiday break so he wouldn't even be walking home from school. But Miguel could still give him an excuse to go back to the garage apartment and talk to her again.

Jake realized, yet again, that he'd lost his mind.

He'd also gone out of his way to avoid Eugene. Their conversation the night before had ended positively and he'd meant what he said about working with him. But his patience was already running thin. If Eugene didn't respond to his offers of assistance better than he had before, Jake would be forced to make a decision that wouldn't sit well with either of them. Jake didn't believe for a minute that Eugene was too old to do his job; in fact, Jake had several other valued employees who were older than Eugene. But Eugene's refusal to adopt new technology and to make any attempt to relate to his security staff was definitely a problem. They had to figure out a way to make it work. Or face the fact that it wasn't going to work at all.

For the day, he didn't want to dwell on any of that. He had neither the compunction nor the focus for big decisions. The only thing his mind seemed willing to do was think about the beautiful young woman he'd met the previous evening.

It wasn't like him at all. At all.

He went home for lunch and did the one thing he promised himself all morning that he absolutely wouldn't do. It was juvenile, sophomoric, stupid. Every mile he drove and every step he took toward his apartment was made with the silent warning not to do it. He congratulated himself when he held off, willing himself to stay away from his laptop, as he made a turkey sandwich and piled some chips on a plate. He grabbed a soda from the fridge, sat on his leather sofa and took a generous bite of the sandwich. The laptop was calling out to him, reminding him of the information it held, the connections it could make.

He took another bite, eyeing the laptop as he would a mortal enemy. He wasn't going to do it. It felt wrong, like spying. He wouldn't stoop to the level of a desperate man on a cheap online dating service, he reminded himself. He wouldn't do it. He was a grown man, he reminded himself over and over as he determined to stick to his guns and then debated about his determination.

He popped the top on his cold soda, took a long pull and then, with a heavy sigh, grabbed the laptop and set it before him on the coffee table. He logged in and, shaking his head in disbelief, he did the one thing he'd decided against all day.

He Googled her.

And he found absolutely nothing. No social media pages with her name, no phone listing or address. He tried the local newspaper. He even conducted a basic property records search using the address of the mansion and found nothing with her name on them. He didn't know how it was possible, but she was the only person in the world who seemed to have absolutely no digital footprint.

Of course, he thought wryly. I know her name and address, and even her child's name, but I can't find one additional fact about her.

Giving up after almost an hour of fruitless searching, he put his plate in the dishwasher, his empty can in the recycling bin and pulled his coat and gloves on. Maybe now that he'd given it the old college try, he could focus on work for the afternoon. There was nothing else for him to do.

Yeah, right. No such luck.

He was making another round through the store. He recognized a few teachers from the high school who were Christmas shopping together. This was their first day of freedom, too. He knew the store would be increasingly busy as parents realized their shopping days were limited and more people took time off from work to prepare for guests and parties. It was one of his favorite times of the year and not just because of the robust sales. He loved the community, the busyness of the season. Jake enjoyed people and the hordes of shoppers brought out the best in him even as they sometimes grew frustrated with the crowds.

He was talking to one of the employees at a register when he had a brilliant idea. Like every other retailer, Crandall's offered gift cards. They had become increasingly popular and were available at every register and through the store's website. He'd tried to convince himself all day that he couldn't get his mind off Cassie and Miguel because of the way the boy had been treated by Eugene. Jake had been horrified when he realized that the older man had a guilty until proven innocent take on the situation and felt even worse when Eugene admitted his mistake. Jake wanted to do something to apologize. A gift card made perfect sense.

He strode back to his office with a purpose and a smile. Once there, he called the director of customer services and asked for a rather generous gift card to be delivered to him. He would take the card to Cassie himself and offer it with another apology. It was a brilliant plan, he congratulated himself.

Within ten minutes, the card was on his desk. He asked his secretary to find one of the special Christmas envelopes they'd printed just for the holiday gift cards. Once she brought it to him, he wrote a quick note and sealed it. Now, he just had to wait for the right time to deliver it.

CHAPTER SIX

"Amen," said a very thankful yet proud Isabella. At four years old, she had already graduated from the rhyming blessings that were usually recited with such speed that they lost meaning. Isabella, Cassie's precious baby girl, was born with a grateful heart even though she'd lost more in her young life than anyone could expect her to comprehend.

Just as Miguel handed his mother a plate heaping with warm tortillas, there was a knock at the door. For a moment, everyone around the table looked at each other with confusion. They never had visitors. Ever.

The knock sounded again, a bit louder. "I'll get it," Miguel bounded up. Cassie placed her hand on his shoulder as she walked behind him.

"I'll get it," she said with a tone that stopped all other ideas. "You eat."

She couldn't imagine who was at their door. She was beat after a long day and still had chores to supervise and lists to make for the rapidly approaching holiday. Isabella was already asking about a Christmas tree.

She opened the door after looking through the peephole, wondering what on earth could have brought him to their doorstep yet again.

"Mr. Crandall?" she asked in greeting. He was tall, so tall she had to look up at him. Snow was salting his dark hair, and he spontaneously shivered in the cold.

"Mrs. Shaw, hello," he began nervously. "I hope I'm not disturbing you and I apologize for not calling. I couldn't find your phone number," he said, his face reddening as if he was embarrassed. Cassie was sure it was from the cold.

"What can I do for you, Mr. Crandall? Is there something else with Miguel?" She could think of no other reason he would make a reappearance at their home. She hadn't had to punish her son after everything that had happened at the store the afternoon before. He'd been so upset that he'd cried into the night. Reassurance was what he'd needed more than discipline.

Jake rubbed his hands together involuntarily. Although he'd worn his heavy wool overcoat and lined leather gloves, the cold was biting.

Cassie took pity on him. "Would you like to step inside?" she asked, opening the door for him.

He smiled and thanked her and took a step inside the tiny cottage. It smelled heavenly. His stomach growled, loud enough for Cassie to hear. Again, color flooded his face. "Please excuse me," he said. "Something smells wonderful."

At that moment, Miguel walked into the room. He'd managed to put yesterday's events behind him but now, seeing Jake at his door, he was sure he was going to jail. At ten years old, he had no idea how the judicial system worked. He knew that he'd been lucky once and his mother always told him that planning on luck was no plan at all. Seeing Jake again, he stopped in his tracks.

"Mama?"

"It's okay Miguel. Go back in the kitchen. I'll be right there," she smiled at him, hoping to reassure him, again, that no one was taking him away from her. Miguel was rooted to the spot.

Sensing the boy's fear, fear that he had caused, Jake immediately began to explain why he'd returned. "I wanted to apologize again. To both of you," he said, looking only at Miguel. He felt miserable about Eugene's allegations and his own part in traumatizing the child. "The security video last night proved Miguel was telling the truth, although I know you believed him anyway. I can't tell you how badly I feel for the way you were treated," he looked at Miguel. Turning to Cassie, he added, "It happened just the way he described. Mr. Winters is a devoted employee and Crandall's is basically all he has in his life. He overreacted."

"Mr. Crandall," Cassie replied. "We've talked about it at length and Miguel understands that mistakes were made all around. Right, Miguel?"

"Yes, ma'am," he responded. He blinked, daring to believe that the apology was real.

"Good. But I've thought about it all day," Jake said. "I know I can't make up for what was done, but I wanted to do something to try to apologize. So," he smiled as he dug through his layers of clothing to find the small envelope with the gift card, "here." He handed it to her proudly, hoping it would help them in some small way.

Cassie looked confused as she opened the envelope. His generosity was startling. And unnecessary.

She handed the envelope back to him. Now he was confused.

"Mr. Crandall, thank you. But no thank you," she said simply.

"I don't understand," he said.

"I'm not sure why you feel the need to offer this, but I can't accept it," she said, looking at the envelope as though it was a snake about to strike.

"I don't understand," Jake repeated.

"What happened yesterday was a misunderstanding. A very unfortunate misunderstanding, but a misunderstanding nonetheless. You apologized. There's nothing else to it," she said.

"Maybe it's over and done with as far as you are concerned," Jake said. "But I was raised to take responsibility for my actions. Mr. Winters is my employee and his actions are mine. My grandfather would be very displeased if I didn't do something to make up for causing the stir we did yesterday. This isn't just from me. It's from my company," he continued to try without success. "If you won't accept it for yourself, please take it for Miguel. He was the most aggrieved yesterday."

"Miguel," she responded, looking sternly at her son, "would not have been aggrieved in the least had he simply followed the rules."

They were at an impasse. He was not taking no for an answer; she was not going to say yes. Jake's mind was revving, trying to come up with a compromise, when the cutest face he'd ever seen peeked around the corner. It was the same little girl who'd advised him about Santa's impending arrival the day before.

"Mama, I need some more milk, please," she said, caught between her own needs and the curiosity she couldn't contain. She eyed Jake from the top of his head to the shoes on his feet.

Cassie laughed, putting her head in her hand. Leave it to Isabella, she thought, to completely drain the tension from the room.

Surprising herself, she said, "Would you like to join us for dinner?"

He was flabbergasted at the offer but recovered quickly. "I'd love to," he said and they all laughed as his stomach rumbled loudly again.

"We're eating very simply tonight. Paella with rice," she said as she led him through the tiny living room into the kitchen. It was small but arranged in a way to make the most out of the space. The appliances, which didn't appear to include a dishwasher, were placed against the back wall. A large island with cabinets had been built practically in the middle of the room and served as extra prep and storage space as well as the dining table. Tall but comfortable stools had been arranged around it. Miguel and Isabella took their usual places as Cassie gestured at an empty stool at the far end of the island. He removed his wool coat and stuffed his gloves in the pockets and hung them on an empty hook on the wall. Two older girls were already seated at the island.

As Cassie pulled an extra place setting from a cabinet and silverware from one of the island's drawers, she said, "Mr. Crandall, these are my other girls, Sophia and Lucia." The girls, each beautiful in her own right, smiled and shook his hand.

Jake hid his surprise well, he thought. Cassie barely looked old enough to have a ten-year old much less two older children. "Everyone, please call me Jake," he smiled.

Cassie spooned a healthy portion of paella, thick with pieces of sausage, chicken and fish in a sauce made from tomatoes, garlic and heavenly seasonings, over Spanish rice. She handed him the plate, and he couldn't contain a groan of pleasure as soon as he tasted it.

"This is absolutely wonderful," he said, piling another bite onto his fork. "Absolutely wonderful."

"It's Lucia's special recipe," Miguel said, smiling at the girl.

"You made this?" he asked her seriously. Jake recalled barely being able to order from a menu when he was a boy. He still wouldn't be able to prepare something as tasty as this dish.

Lucia nodded, grinning. "I like to make it," she said. "It's pretty easy and everybody likes it." She handed him the plate with tortillas as Cassie placed a glass of iced tea in front of him.

The tortillas were warm and pillow soft. "Lucia made those, too," Isabella offered, poking a hole in the middle of one and twirling it on her small finger.

"You are a very gifted chef," Jake smiled at Lucia. "You have a great future in the culinary arts," he added, as she smiled proudly. She always loved a compliment.

Dinner was a long affair in the Shaw household that night. They weren't used to having guests join them. Jake asked about school and books they liked. He asked them what they liked to do for fun and what kind of music they were into. They asked him about the store, and he told them funny stories about people shopping for Christmas. He had them all laughing uproariously when he told them about the year a squirrel ran into the store and climbed up the Christmas tree.

After a while, Cassie said, "Okay, it's time to finish your chores everybody." Without a complaint, all four children rose from the table, collected their plates as well as Cassie's and Jake's, and cleared the island.

Sophia, the oldest, began washing the dishes after she put away the leftovers. Lucia took a laundry basket stored beside the stacked washer and dryer and filled it with clothes ready to be sorted, folded and put away. Isabella made sure all the trash was in the waste can and that everyone had hung their coat on an assigned hook and placed their gloves, hats and shoes neatly in a bin below. Miguel grabbed his jacket from his assigned hook and was pulling his gloves on when he said, "Mama, I have a great idea! I think Jake should go to the ice rink with us!"

The girls were overjoyed with the idea. Isabella jumped up and down, clapping her hands and cheering, "Yay, Jake! Yay, Jake!" over and over again.

Cassie was clearly not as thrilled with the suggestion as the children had been. "Mr. Crandall," she began, "I mean Jake, is a very busy man. I'm sure he doesn't have time to go to the ice rink with us." Even to her own ears, she sounded sterner than she'd intended.

She was right, of course. Jake was a busy man. Other than the day after Thanksgiving, the next few days would be the busiest of the year for him. There would be special orders and deliveries and at least one salesperson would have a meltdown. They would run out of change at every register at least twice a day. Shoppers would either be happy or harried, leisurely or frantic, patient or wild. He would be needed virtually around the clock.

He looked at the five faces, four of them staring hopefully at him. He looked at Cassie and said, "When are you going? I have plenty of time."

Countdown: 4 days until Christmas

CHAPTER SEVEN

Jake couldn't remember the last time he'd been ice skating. Years, at least. And still, he was the resident expert of the group. He and Cassie tied laces for the girls and Miguel as they laughed nervously, excited for the experience and afraid of falling.

Once everyone was laced up, Jake led them one by one to the edge of the rink and instructed them to hold onto the fence around it. They lined up like ducks with Jake in the lead and Cassie in the back, ready to catch and soothe as best she could.

"Okay, everyone, here's the thing," Jake said, "Falling is part of learning when it comes to skating. Once you get the hang of it, it will be like flying. But you have to try to fly. Got it?" They all nodded.

"I'll take one at a time around the rink. The rest of you, hold onto the fence like this and move your feet back and forth like this." He showed them how to shuffle their feet just to get used to the feeling of their skates on the surface. He told them that they didn't have to wait their turn with him but could take off on their own if they wanted to. The invitation was met with white-knuckled grips on the fence.

"Okay, then," he said, "C'mon Bella, let's show them how it's done." The little girl clapped gleefully. As the youngest, she was not usually the first to try new things. She was ready and the least nervous of the group. Jake had noticed and hoped that the others would feel the pressure to join in once they saw their little sister skating around on her own. He had no doubt she would pick it up quickly.

He was right. After he'd toured Bella around the rink twice, she was ready to let go of his hand and take off. Even when she fell, which was rare, she laughed and tried again immediately. "Okay, who's next?" Jake asked.

Within fifteen minutes, all four children were skating on their own. They didn't look like professionals, but they were doing okay and having a tremendous time.

"Okay, Cassie, your turn," he said, with a wide grin as he held his hand out to her.

"I think I might just go sit over there and watch everyone," she said, biting her lower lip nervously.

"Oh, I don't think so," he said, pulling her gently away from the fence. "You can't let a bunch of kids show you up. You'll never hear the end of it."

She knew he was right. They would tease her unmercifully if she didn't at least try to skate. She took his hand and let him lead her around the rink slowly.

"Mama, look at me!" Bella exclaimed as she flew by them. Miguel was close behind, becoming braver with every turn. Sophia and Lucia were much more cautious. At their ages, they were more concerned with how they looked than they were about becoming good skaters.

"Okay, if you want to sit down now, I think your pride will remain intact," Jake said to her. They'd been around the rink a half-dozen times and her kids had commented on her bravery. They thought it was cool that she had tried.

"You think so?" she asked with a smile. It was one of the few times she had smiled so completely that it reached her eyes. When he saw it, Jake's heart melted a little bit. He led her to a wooden bench close to the rink but out of the direct line of fire of any out-of-control skaters. They sat and watched for a few minutes, laughing at the antics of her children and the other skaters.

"Thank you for coming today," Cassie finally broke the comfortable silence. "They learned so much more quickly with you," she smiled.

"You don't have to thank me," Jake replied. I've had a great time."

They both had on thick jackets, jeans and boots, caps and gloves. They were bundled up against the wind and cold but it made real conversation difficult. Mostly, they sat in silence and laughed at the kids and the other brave souls making their way around the rink.

After a while, Cassie said, "My kids haven't laughed like this in a long time." She sounded, at least to Jake, almost sad about the fact that her children were having fun. He had no idea what the source of that sadness was, but he wanted to know. And he wanted to remove it from her life.

"You sound almost sad that they are having a good time," he said gently, hoping to prompt more discussion. He'd learned quickly from their previous conversations that she was very guarded, always observing. It was one of the few things he knew about her.

"I'm not at all sad that they are having fun," she said. "I wish they had more opportunity to just be carefree. They've had serious lives already," she said. It was a matter-of-fact statement, and her face showed little emotion.

Just as he was about to pry, and he realized that's what it was, Bella came bounding up to them, her tiny nose red from the cold. Her hair was in pigtails and her jacket, hat, socks and sweater were all bright pink. She looked exactly like a sweet little girl who would be a princess should look, and he couldn't stop grinning at her.

"Mama, I can do a circle," she cried as she threw her hands up in victory. "And I can almost do it without falling down!"

Cassie and Jake laughed and clapped for her and promised to watch. She ran back to the rink and stopped right in front of them. With a studious countenance, she crossed one skate over the other and spun. And immediately fell down. Still, they clapped and shouted congratulations as she tried again and again.

The older girls found some friends from school and talked with them as they skated slowly while managing to stay upright. Miguel was a natural and was skating around everyone else on the rink. Jake felt a surge of pride at having had a hand in teaching them the basics.

He had to take a few calls from the store, but nothing too urgent had happened so far. The fact that he could manage it and have fun with Cassie and her kids at the same time was astounding. And freeing.

They stayed for a couple of hours, and everyone had a wonderful time. Jake returned their skates to the vendor. As he rejoined their group, he overheard them talking about being hungry. It was little wonder since they had been working hard on the rink while wearing at least ten pounds of clothes and gear.

"I have an idea," he said. He was taking a chance because he knew how Cassie felt about accepting charity. "Do you guys like pizza?"

"Yeah!" came the immediate response from the back of Cassie's minivan. "Pizz-a! Pizz-a! Pizz-a!" they began cheering. He was sitting in the passenger seat and he cast a glance at Cassie to judge her reaction. She tried to look mad at him for asking the kids before he asked her, but she couldn't hold it. Pizza was an inexpensive treat that her kids loved. She finally grinned as she rolled her eyes. There was no way she could say no.

"I know a place," he said. "Turn right at the light."

Within minutes they were trooping into a small, family-owned restaurant known for its pizza and pasta.

"Well, look what the cat dragged in," shouted a man with a mop of unruly blond hair and a mile-wide smile. He was broad-shouldered and tall, a man who could be described as "bigger than life." He was wearing a bibbed apron more red from sauce than white. "Hey, man, where you been?" he asked Jake as he grabbed him in a bear hug.

"Working, man, working. It is the holiday season, you know. A poor retailer's bread and butter." They slapped each other on the shoulder and took a moment to catch up.

"So, my friend here has clearly forgotten his manners," the man said to Cassie and the kids. "I'm Tony and I welcome you to Pouncy's, my family's humble eating establishment." He smiled at them all and shook Cassie's hand when Jake introduced her. "You look like a group of hungry pizza eaters to me, am I right?"

"Yeah! Pizz-a! Pizz-a! Pizz-a!"

"Right this way. Don't worry about menus. You just tell me what you want," Tony said as he led them to a large round table covered with a plastic checkered tablecloth. In the middle of the table sat a Lazy Susan with a pile of clean napkins, a shaker of fresh Parmesan cheese and another filled with hot pepper flakes. The children settled on a couple of pizzas while Jake and Cassie ordered pasta. Tony brought around drinks and then gave the kids a handful of coins to play the retro video games set up along one wall.

"Let me know if you guys had rather a glass of wine than soft drinks," Tony said as the children scattered off.

Jake looked at Cassie with raised eyebrows in question. "I'm driving," she said simply.

"We're good," Jake said to Tony. "Thanks."

Tony sauntered off to greet new arrivals, wipe off the tables and take care of the general business of running a family restaurant.

Cassie looked relaxed, Jake thought. He wondered how often she was able to do that. He had no idea where the kids' father was but he hadn't been around, nor had Cassie called him all day. Jake was more than a little curious but he sensed that if he tried to find out too much too fast, he would lose any chance he might have to get to know her better. It was safe to talk about her children, whom she obviously adored, and Jake didn't mind at all. Throughout the day, Jake had managed to spend time with each of them and thought they were incredible children. They had laughed at and with each other all day without a cross word or hurt feeling. Although he was an only child and had no experience in the sibling department, he thought this was a minor miracle.

"You have given them a great day," Cassie said to him. "Thank you for that."

"Hey, I've had a great time, too. I haven't been skating in forever. In fact, I haven't played outside in forever," he smiled. "And Tony's pizza is the best in the world. It's the secret to my undergraduate success, in fact," he said.

"Really? Do tell," she smiled back.

He regaled her with stories from his college days when he and Tony, a boyhood friend who had talked his parents into sending him to college, would raid the restaurant's kitchen after hours as they studied or partied. More than once, the police had shown up when the boys forgot to turn off the silent alarm. They never had much trouble, however, once they'd offered the responding officers a slice or two of the neighborhood's best cheese pie.

They were laughing together when Tony brought their food to the table. As Cassie went to round up the kids, Tony asked, "So what's with the Brady Bunch act, dude?"

"Long story," Jake replied. "And the short version is I have no idea what I'm doing."

"As usual," Tony slapped Jake on the back with a chuckle as the group returned, jockeying for position to sit close to Jake. Miguel sat so close to him that that were almost sharing a chair as he told him about the video games he played, the same games that Jake had played years before.

"And then, this space ship was like 'phew, phew, phew' and I hit it with my rockets and then I got double rockets and it was awesome!" Miguel was shouting above the din. Jake laughed at the boy's excitement as Cassie tried to serve pizza to everyone, move glasses out of the way and gain some sense of calm.

She finally gave up and joined in the oohing and aahing over the food. She had to admit that her lasagna was excellent and the fact that she hadn't had to prepare it made it taste even better.

Between them, they ate every bite and scrap of their food. Completely stuffed, they bundled up in their cold weather gear, waved goodbye to Tony and headed out. By the time they reached their street, everyone was warm from the car's heater and quiet. Bedtime, Cassie knew, would be mercifully early.

They ambled inside their small house and before they could hang their coats, gloves and hats on their hooks in the kitchen, Cassie instructed them that everyone needed a five minute shower before they put their pajamas on.

Sophia volunteered to supervise Bella who usually preferred a bath over a shower. But the little girl was so tired that she could hardly hold her eyes open so she headed to the bathroom without an argument.

"Would you like some coffee?" Cassie asked him. He was blowing on his hands to warm them up.

"I don't want to be too much trouble," he said as his eyes pleaded for a warm drink.

"It's no trouble," Cassie chuckled. "I'm making some for

myself. Would you mind lighting the fire?" she asked.

"No, not at all," he answered, grateful for something to keep busy with. The day had been easy, easier than he would have imagined. While they had shared no secrets or dreams, their talks had been companionable. There were a million questions he wanted to ask her. He was still nervous but was growing more comfortable sharing space and time with her.

By the time the fire was lit and the coffee brewed, the children had said their good-nights. Jake thought they'd all be asleep before their heads hit their pillows. Cassie, too, was probably tired.

He sat on one end of a small couch and took in the details around the room. There were family pictures, most of them un-posed and funny. A few small rocks were stacked carefully on a side table, treasures he suspected from an adventurous walk. The curtains were beautiful, not fine but well-made and colorful. The hardwood floors gleamed as did every bit of wood on the furniture. There were trinkets here and there and a wooden mantel with various sizes of candles across it. Nothing in the room was expensive but it was all well-cared for and put together with an eye for comfortable design. He felt more at home here than he'd ever felt in his own apartment's living room.

Cassie entered the room with a serving tray loaded with a small carafe, two steaming mugs of coffee and cream and sugar in tiny serving pieces. It was a sign of a woman who loved to entertain. She placed them on the square coffee table in front of the couch. Like many of the pieces he'd seen, the table looked as though it had been carefully repurposed. Before she joined him on the sofa, she pulled a knitting project from a hidden drawer in the side of the coffee table.

"I hope you don't mind," she smiled. "I'm still finishing up some Christmas presents and I don't usually have this much quiet this early in the evening."

"Of course I don't mind," he smiled back. He added a bit of sugar and cream to his coffee and took a drink. It was perfect, just strong enough to make him wake up and take notice. The excitement of the day, the exercise at the rink and the heavy dinner were making him as sleepy as the kids had been.

"So what are you making?" he asked her.

"A sweater for Miguel," she said. "He's growing so fast I can hardly keep him in clothes," she laughed. "I'm purposefully making this a bit big and I hope it will see him through the entire winter."

The click-clacking of the knitting needles were soothing, a steady staccato in the otherwise quiet room.

"I have to tell you that I've never seen children as well-behaved as yours," he said honestly. He was thinking about their day and the lack of fussing and feuding between the four. "I'd always thought that doing anything with four children would require a dog whistle and a rosary at least," he chuckled. "I had fun with them,"

She laughed. "They are good kids most of the time," she smiled. "But don't be fooled. They are still kids. They like to push the limits at times as I expect they always will. It hasn't been easy for any of them, but I try to keep them busy."

"What hasn't been easy?" he asked, placing his cup back on the saucer. "I don't mean to pry if you don't want to talk about it," he retreated seeing the look of doubt that crossed her face.

"I haven't had anyone to really talk with for a long time," she said. The furious needles stopped quickly as she stopped counting rows and looked into the fire as if watching a movie. "It's funny how quickly you can become used to being lonely," she said quietly.

Jake sat in silence, not sure what to say.

"My husband died three years ago, when Bella was just

a year old. He was in the Army, in the Middle East for his second tour. He loved serving. Not in some wild cowboy, shoot 'em up kind of way. He loved the calling to serve, the chance to make something better," she said. "Of course, we'd always known it was a possibility - that he could get wounded or killed. It's just something you have to accept. Still, I was in shock when I found out."

"I imagine so," Jake said. He knew the feeling and knew it well.

"Miguel was devastated," she continued. "He wouldn't eat or sleep. I eventually had to pull him out of school because he would just sit, completely withdrawn. It took longer than a year for him to pull out of it." Tears gathered in her eyes at the memory of her son's despair. She would never be able to completely put that time out of her mind, she knew. That particular wound would always be a part of her.

She turned back to her knitting. "My sister brought her two girls, Lucia and Sophia, here, and they lived with us. I don't know if I could have made it without her."

"They're your nieces?" Jake asked. "Well, that actually makes more sense."

She looked at him in confusion.

"I couldn't imagine that you are old enough to have a sixteen year old," he smiled.

"Thank you," she replied sincerely as she blushed.

"Where is your sister now?"

"Her husband had an accident at work. He worked in construction in Mexico, mostly on the resorts. Their government is trying to recreate the tourism industry that's taken such a hit over the past few years. To me, it's like putting lipstick on a pig but whatever. Matias had more than enough work which isn't always the case there. He was on some scaffolding and fell. He broke his back. They've had a long, hard road but are still optimistic."

Jake sat, astounded at all she had told him. Their family had certainly had more than their fair share of heartbreak and tragedy.

"I can't imagine how hard it's been for all of you," he said gently. Their coffee had grown cold, but neither of them noticed. She seemed to be making great progress on the sweater she held in her hands as they talked. "How have you handled it all?"

"Faith. God. Church. Prayer. Whatever you want to call it, it's what we've leaned on and how we've gotten through," she said it so matter-of-factly that he didn't dare question her. He'd religiously attended three church services every year: Christmas, Easter and Mother's Day. Other than that, faith wasn't something he gave much thought about. Except when they routinely said the blessing at a family dinner or, sometimes, in traffic.

"So why did you stay here instead of going to Mexico with your sister?" he asked. He was curious and wanted to know everything he could find out about her. He also wanted to change the subject.

"The children. They all have a much better chance of staying in school, of even staying safe here. The resort Matias was working on is in a remote area of the country and much of it is still undeveloped. The girls' dad was born in Mexico, but Elena and I were born here as was my husband. Staying after my brother-in-law's accident was one of the hardest decisions I've ever made. Elena needed me as much as I had needed her. Her girls miss her and their father like crazy. But they have access to so much more here than they would in Mexico, especially with one parent injured and unable to work," she explained.

She smiled at him. "Lucia has already started a successful business doing graphic design and computer tutoring. Sophia is a tremendous seamstress and fashion designer, even at her age, and I want to encourage them both in business. I know they are young but they have a passion and talent. I want them to be independent and to be able to provide for themselves."

He sat silently for a moment, taking it all in. "That's amazing. I still don't feel ready to take over my family's business and I'm twice their age!" They both laughed. Cassie assumed he was joking. Jake was completely serious.

"And what do you do?" he asked. They'd talked quite a bit during the day but most of it had been about children or funny stories that didn't divulge a lot of personal information.

"I'm a paralegal," she said.

"I'm impressed," he answered. It wasn't a compliment he just tossed out and he wanted her to know that. "I had to deal with a few lawyers when I turned twenty-one and when my grandfather turned the store over to me," he explained. "I actually spent more time with their staff, including their paralegals, than I did with the lawyers."

"Oh, well then you know a little about what I do," she smiled. "Most people have no idea. I work hard at getting better and learning more. It's difficult when my colleagues can work longer hours than I can to stay at the top in my law firm. The kids are my priority, though, and my bosses know that."

"Have you thought about law school?" he asked.

"I have. In fact, like a lot of people, I became a paralegal to get some experience in the legal field and to test the waters. Law school is long and expensive, and I don't have the resources to spend if I don't think I'll love it."

"And?"

"Yes, I think I would love to be a lawyer so I dream of going to law school. Maybe someday," she said as the knitting needles moved even faster. She couldn't believe she was telling him so much about herself. She hadn't revealed so much about her hopes and dreams to anyone since her husband died.

"And what about you?" she asked, stilling the needles and stretching her hands. They had been furiously working for virtually their entire conversation.

"What about me?" he asked as if he was a completely open book. It wasn't exactly the truth and she could sense it.

"Wife? Siblings? Parents? Do you like running Crandall's? What's your story?" she asked. "Turn about is fair play, you know."

"I've never been married," he began, leaning forward with his elbows on his knees, "I don't have any brothers or sisters and always wanted one of each. My mother died when I was two, and my father died before that. My grandparents raised me, and I still spend a lot of time with them. When my grandfather was ready to retire, we all knew I would take over the store."

"Do you like doing that?"

"Honestly? I love it. I've always felt like I had a place there. I'm still trying to figure out how to do it my way. I don't want people to forget all that my grandfather did to make it a success. That's really important to me."

"That's understandable," she said.

"You think so?" He wasn't sure he agreed. His grandparents kept telling him he had free reign. He believed them. He just couldn't bring himself to make big changes. At least not yet.

"You've had as much pain as we have. It's not always easy to welcome change when so much has been forced on you," she said with compassion. Sometimes it was easy to forget that other people had gone through as much heartache as she had. She had taken on so much responsibility early in her life, more than she thought possible. But Jake had plenty on his shoulders as well. Maybe that explained why she'd felt like he was a kindred spirit from the first time they met.

"I've always wished I could remember my parents," he

said, looking into the fire. "I don't know whether it would have been easier or not but I've always felt like I was missing something. Don't get me wrong, my grandparents are absolutely wonderful, and I love them but it's just different, I think."

"I understand, sort of anyway. I'm doing all I can to be mother and father to the children. Most days, I feel like I fail miserably," she said with a shrug. She'd gone back to knitting, and he noticed that when she talked about herself, she knitted. When they were talking about him, she gave him her full attention.

"Are you kidding?" he gasped. "Those kids are amazing. I honestly don't know how you do it," he smiled genuinely.

"Everyone pitches in," she answered with another shrug.

"Yes, but four kids in a pretty small space? Four kids on one salary? Four kids?" He didn't know how she remained calm in the midst of all her responsibilities.

She laughed. "I guess you get used to it. They help me and each other a lot. We live here because it's free - although it does cost a fortune to keep it heated through the winter - and I'm afraid we will have to move soon anyway. It's not fair to the girls that they all have to stay in one room but Miguel is too old to share with any of them. Someday, I might actually want to sleep in a real bed," she laughed again.

"Where do you sleep now?"

"We are actually sitting on my bed," she chuckled. Without thinking, he took a big gulp from his coffee cup and grimaced at the bitter taste.

"Would you like for me to warm that up for you?" she laughed.

He shook his head as if to shake off his rebelling taste buds. "No, that's okay. It's getting late. I could sit and talk to you all night," he said, honestly. "But tomorrow will be a big day at the store. The countdown is on, after all." He stood and retrieved his coat from a chair beside the fireplace. It was warm from the fire and would feel good as soon as he walked outside.

"Listen, I have an idea. I know you didn't want to accept the gift card I brought by. I still wish you would, but I understand," he said quickly as she crossed her arms. "But how about this? Every big business gives its employees a Christmas bonus, right? I think your kids deserve one, too. I know they don't work for me, but they do work. So what if I give them our employee discount for anything they want to buy at the store? You said they earn their own money so they can spend their hard-earned cash. I'll just make it go a little further. They can get presents for each other or their parents or you or their friends. Whatever they want. Could we do that?" he asked. He'd bundled up again, ready to head out the door.

"Can I think about it?" she asked. She wanted to do the right thing and she wasn't so sure why he wanted to make such a gesture for the kids.

"Of course. If you decide to take me up on it, just come by the store. I'll be there around the clock for the next couple of days," he said. He was actually looking forward to it. He loved this time of year.

"Okay, and thank you. I don't know why you're doing this but I really do appreciate it," she said, opening the door for him.

"I'm a nice guy," he said with a smile. "I had a great time today. Thanks for letting me tag along."

"You were the life of the party!" she laughed.

There was an awkward moment as he left. It felt as though they had become friends, close friends, in a twenty-four hour span. It was unlike both of them.

Jake wanted to hug her. He wanted to reassure her that

she was doing a great job with the kids and that she now had someone to talk with when she was sad or overwhelmed. He wanted to be there for her more than he'd wanted to be around for anyone in a long time.

    Instead of reaching for her, he nodded and headed out into the dark, cold night. She returned their coffee cups and tray to the kitchen and put everything away before she warmed another cup in the microwave and returned to her knitting. She could finish most of Miguel's sweater before she went to bed, she thought. If, she took a deep breath and tried to refocus, she could concentrate on it instead of the man who'd just walked out of her house.

Countdown: 3 days until Christmas

CHAPTER EIGHT

It was so late when Cassie finally went to sleep that she slept on the couch without unfolding the bed. As a result, her muscles ached when she awoke. She'd dreamed all night about her family. Her husband and she were walking along a beautiful boulevard. In France, perhaps. Flowers of every color lined the sidewalks, and they walked under the bluest sky and whitest clouds she'd ever seen. It was idyllic, truly. She didn't know what they were talking about, but they laughed easily as they strolled along holding hands. They reached a bridge and looked down at the water. It was stunningly blue and calm, the kind of water that made you want to jump in with your clothes on and laugh yourself silly. They stood there for a few moments, watching the water and breathing in the clear air. Her husband reached down and plucked a single flower, handed it to her and kissed her hand. Then, with a smile, he walked across the bridge alone. In her dream, she stood and watched him walk away, waved and then turned and walked back down the boulevard. The sun continued to shine and a warm breeze blew across her face and hair.

She awoke with a start, puzzled about the dream. Her husband had seemed as real as if he had been beside her on the couch. But he'd been gone for years. The more she let herself feel the way through the dream, it was as though he had visited to be sure she was finding happiness and feeling peaceful.

The dream was bittersweet. To see him, touch him, share with him again was so wonderful. He smiled all the way to his eyes, just like he had when he was alive. But she'd known, even in the dream, that it wasn't real and that he couldn't stay. To have him so close was too good to be true. And, in fact, it wasn't true at all.

She sat on the couch and folded the blanket she'd pulled over her legs during the night. She rubbed the sleep out of her eyes and realized she was hungry. The smell of brewed coffee and cooking bacon called her into the kitchen. She checked the clock on the wall and saw that she'd slept, uncharacteristically, until almost eight.

"Good morning," she said, dropping a kiss on Lucia's head and rubbing Sophia's back tenderly. "You guys are awfully productive this morning."

"The kids are sleeping," Sophia replied, "but we know there's a lot to do today. We thought bacon might work. It usually does." They smiled together. Everyone knew that bacon was the key to starting Miguel and Bella's day off in the right direction.

"How did you girls sleep?" she asked, pulling plates from a cabinet and setting the island/table.

"I was so tired," Lucia said as she stretched. "Skating was so much fun but it is hard work!"

"Listen," Cassie said to them. She'd decided on the spur of the moment to share Jake's generous offer with them. "I know you both have been working hard and saving money. And you know," she looked them in the eye one at a time to emphasize her next words, "that you do not need to buy Christmas presents for the three of us."

She waited until they each nodded their understanding before she continued. "Last night, Jake and I were talking and he admires both of you. Very much, in fact. He's intrigued by your business ideas and your hard work. So he offered to let both of you shop at Crandall's with a full employee discount. I don't know if there's anything you still need to get, and I would encourage you both, if there's anything you'd like for yourself, to think about getting some treat with that discount. You both deserve it."

"He can do that?" Lucia asked, astonished.

"Yes, he can. He owns the store," Cassie said simply. She thought they understood this.

"The whole store?" she asked again.

"Yes, silly," Sophia said, not willing to miss an opportunity to show off her older-sister sophistication. "He owns the whole store and everything in it." She looked conspiratorially at Cassie and subtly rolled her eyes. Then she asked, "It's okay if we spend it on anything? Anything at all?"

"Well, yes," Cassie said, wondering if she'd made a mistake. The girls were usually very responsible with their money because they knew how hard it was to earn. "If you want to take him up on his offer, you should figure out how much you can afford to spend and stick to that budget."

"Okay, thanks," they both answered. They went back to working together seamlessly to finish preparing breakfast and put everything on the table. They were obviously already thinking about what they might buy at the department store they didn't usually visit.

"Okay," Cassie said, "I hear the pitter-patter of little warriors coming to claim their bacon. And we have a lot to do today."

"Like getting a Christmas tree!" Bella yelled at the top of her lungs, running through the kitchen like she'd been shot out of a canon.

Cassie couldn't help it. She laughed riotously with the others. She just couldn't discipline such joy. Sometimes everyone except Bella thought too much about all they'd lost. Bella, because she was too young to remember any of the tragedy, was full-on ready for Christmas. Any day of the year. Cassie swooped her up and gave her a big kiss before firmly planting her on one of the stools at the island. Bella was breathless with excitement.

"Mommy, Mommy, Mommy!" she yelled. "Christmas is in this many days!" She held up three tiny fingers. Each word was louder than the one before so that they all felt the need to cover their ears with their hands.

"Okay, who let the cat out of the bag?" Cassie looked at the older children with a mock scowl. They'd all agreed to keep the counting down to a minimum for their mental health and general well-being. The year before, Bella had begun the countdown to Christmas right after the Fourth of July.

"It was me," Miguel said, looking down at his plate. "She was so ramnuxious at the pizza place that I told her she had to behave or Santa wouldn't come to see her."

Cassie hid her grin behind her napkin until she could continue to act seriously. "First, the word is rambunctious and, second, she would have found out today anyway." She sighed heavily as if something terrible was on her mind. She looked at each of the children before continuing. "I mean she'd know something was up when we pick out a Christmas tree today."

When she couldn't contain it any longer, a huge grin spread across her face. The kids began to cheer and laugh with her. They weren't used to Cassie being so relaxed and funny. They'd forgotten how nice it was when they didn't have to be on such a rigid schedule for work and school. And they knew she'd had fun yesterday, too, on their rare day out.

Sophia pulled two cookie sheets out of the oven and placed a stack of hot waffles on a platter. She placed it beside a plate with a heaping pile of bacon. Lucia had warmed the syrup and put the butter on the island. Coffee and milk were poured, and the group devoured the breakfast as if they hadn't eaten in years.

"Sophia, these are the best waffles in the whole world," Bella said around a mouthful, syrup dripping down her tiny chin.

"Why, thank you, Bella Button," the older girl replied with a smile. The two of them, the oldest and the youngest, had always had a very special bond. When Cassie's husband died, there had been so much worry with Miguel that Bella, only a baby at the time, fell into the care of Cassie's sister and her girls. Sophia had been with Bella every minute that she could. When she'd learned to sew and mend clothes so beautifully, she'd found some big buttons at a thrift store, and she'd tied them together with a pink ribbon for Bella to play with. It quickly became her favorite toy and the nickname "Bella Button" was born. Sophia was the only person still allowed to call her that.

"Okay, so here's the plan," Cassie said. "We are going to finish the best waffles in the world and clean up the kitchen. Then we are going to get dressed and go find a Christmas tree. Don't forget you all have pageant practice this afternoon so we'll do that and then we will come home and decorate. How does that sound?"

For what seemed like the sixtieth time that morning, they all cheered. It warmed Cassie's heart to see them all smiling and healthy and whole. Two years ago, she wouldn't have believed it could be possible. They had felt bereft, lost and alone. But they weren't. They had never been alone.

Cassie would never, ever forget the day when Miguel came to her. She was going through the classifieds, trying to find a job when she sensed him there. He hadn't announced his presence in months and talked only when it was absolutely necessary. It was like living with two ghosts in the house: her dead husband's and her living son's.

"Mom," he said, coming to sit next to her on the couch. She dropped the newspaper she'd been reading immediately. She looked into the eyes of her baby, dark circles under a child's eyes was not normal, but the worry and sadness he bore had put them there.

"Yes, baby, what is it?" She sat back on the couch and took his hand. Although he'd withdrawn verbally, he still welcomed touches and hugs.

"I'm not going to be sad anymore," he said simply. His face was as impassive as it had been for months. Only by his words would she have known he wasn't incredibly sad.

"I'm glad to hear that," she said. He sat beside her, and she pulled his tiny body close to hers and hugged him close to her side. They sat quietly for a couple of minutes.

"Do you want to know why?" he whispered.

"Yes," she whispered back. "I really do."

"Because Daddy is in heaven," he said. He was looking her straight in the eye. "If he can't be with us, I know he would want to be there with God. Those are the only places Daddy would be happy, right?"

Tears fell unchecked down her face as she hugged him again. She hugged him so tight she heard him inhale sharply. All the Bible verses about the wisdom and faith of children flew through her mind.

She wiped her face with her sleeve and looked at her son. "Yes, sweetheart, I believe the two places Daddy would be happiest are here with us and heaven."

"So, if Daddy is happy, I should be happy." For Miguel, it had come down to a matter of faith, although he was far too young to realize or appreciate that fact. It had taken him a long time to work through it, but he had. And he'd come to a conclusion that most adults would have a hard time understanding.

He hadn't jumped right back into life that day; it still took some time. Even now, Cassie would see a certain sadness in his eyes and know he was thinking about his father. But he could also talk about him with a smile. It would always be hard for him. But he had the foundation of love to deal with it. And though it broke Cassie's heart that he would forever hurt in a way she didn't have the power to heal, she wouldn't change the love Miguel and his father had felt for each other for anything in the world.

It had been their love and faith that pulled them through, kept them together and made them whole again. Even though times were still tough, they still had that faith, love and each other. It was on full display at the breakfast table as they laughed and planned, and Bella, before the tree was even purchased, declared it to be the "best Christmas tree in the whole world!"

CHAPTER NINE

Bundled up against the weather and singing Christmas carols, they piled into the minivan and headed to their church where a Christmas tree stand had been erected. It had become an annual fundraiser and outreach program for the small church, and everyone in the neighborhood looked forward to it. It was only minutes from their house so the drive was quick. The parking lot was full, and Cassie could hear the speakers blaring carols before she turned off the engine.

Several men in the congregation had grown beards to work the stand, and they had all dressed like Santa or Paul Bunyan, depending on their age and hair color. There was a small booth in the middle of the trees where hot chocolate flowed, and warm cookies were served. Music blasted and thousands of tiny clear lights were strung everywhere making it seem like a whimsical party even in midday.

"Hey, Cassie!" she heard someone call. She turned to see a man with a broad smile walking toward her. She recognized him but wasn't sure how.

"It's Tony, from Pouncy's Pizza," he reminded her as he approached with an offered handshake.

"Of course," she laughed as they shook hands. "I'm sorry I didn't recognize you."

"No big deal," he said good-naturedly. "I might forget a face, but I never forget a pizza. Right, cheese eaters?" he said to Miguel and Bella. They laughed at him. Sophia and Lucia were talking with friends from church who were volunteering at the tree stand.

"Have you seen Jake?" Tony asked her.

"No. I imagine he's working today," she smiled.

"Yes, he has been working, and he will immediately return to work," he explained, rubbing his hands together in the cold. "But his grandmother is insistent that we bring a Christmas tree to her this morning. Says she's running out of time to decorate. Which I guess is true," he shrugged. "We come here every year. She thinks we go out to their farm and cut down one of their own, but we've been coming here for years."

Cassie laughed. "Are you serious? That's cheating!"

She was glad that Bella and Miguel had moved to the edge of the trees and were building a small snowman. If Bella heard the word "cheating," they were all in for a speech about the virtues of truth-telling in every situation.

"No, it's not," he defended. "It's getting a wonderful woman what she wants in the most efficient manner possible." He even crossed his heart with one hand as if he were a knight doing a fair lady's bidding.

"You should have been a lawyer," she said, grinning.

"There you are," Jake said as he jogged toward Tony.

"Well, hey there," he grinned when he saw Cassie. "What are you doing here?"

"Really?" she answered with a laugh and a raised eyebrow.

"Oh, yeah," he said, tucking his head in embarrassment. She was standing in a Christmas tree lot, and her four children were all around. Her purpose was obvious.

"I hear you're here to pull off the annual Great Christmas Tree Scam," she chided.

"Us?" he answered, laughing. "Surely you wouldn't accuse two pillars of the community of something so...so...so dastardly."

Tony's laugh barked out. "'Dastardly'? Seriously dude?"

"I thought it went well with 'scam,'" Jake replied.

"Jake, Jake, Jake!" Bella cried. She and Miguel had

spotted him and they both ran up to him. Bella threw herself into his arms as if they hadn't seen him in years. He couldn't think of anything that had given him so much joy in his life.

"Beautiful Bella," he said, returning her hug and setting her gently on the ground beside Miguel. "Miguel, my friend," he added, slapping hands in a cool, manly way he thought appropriate for a boy Miguel's age.

"Come and see our snowman," Bella yelled as she tugged him by the hand. The kids had done an admirable job, Jake thought, given their heights and ages.

"Wow, this is great," he said. "But why isn't he talking?"

"Talking?" Bella laughed as if it was the most ridiculous question she'd ever heard. "Snowmen can't talk!"

"Then how do they order hot chocolate?" he asked her.

"He can't drink hot stuff, silly. He would melt!"

"Oh, yeah. You're right. I guess we'd better keep him over here away from the fire," he grinned. "How about you? Do you like hot chocolate?" She was the cutest kid he'd ever seen.

"Not too much. It burns my mouth," she explained. "But," she added with a manipulative grin, "I love chocolate chip cookies."

"Huh. You do? That really surprises me," he said. Miguel rolled his eyes.

They returned to Tony and Cassie who had been lost in talk about the restaurant and his hopes to open a second location.

"So, have you found the perfect tree yet?" Jake asked Cassie.

She laughed. "We haven't even started looking yet!"

"I thought maybe, and this is totally up to you, of course, but I was thinking that if these guys helped you find the perfect tree, we could load it up for you and then maybe, just maybe, I could possibly, just maybe, find some really good chocolate chip cookies and hot chocolate for us."

"Yay, yay, yay!" Bella cried. Jake had already learned to expect just this kind of reaction. In fact, he'd hoped for it.

"Well, Bella obviously needs some sugar," Cassie said with another laugh. "Let me find the other girls, and we'll start the hunt for the tree to end all trees."

They located the older girls, and the hunt was on for two perfect trees. They circled the entire lot at least twice, with Bella announcing that each and every tree was perfect and the only one she wanted. They laughed at her unabashed delight.

"Okay, boss," Tony said to Jake. "We need to make a decision. Your grandmother will be worried if we don't bring her a tree and soon."

"I like that Fraser Fir over there," he said, pointing to a tree that was at least ten feet tall. "I think she'd be pleased with that."

"Me too," Tony said, "but just in case, I'll get a smaller version, too." He went to find one of the volunteers to pay and help them load their trees into his truck.

"So what about you guys? See anything you like?" Jake asked Cassie and her group.

"Girls, what do you think?" she asked Lucia and Sophia. They had been quiet during the trip, as usual. Jake knew that they both had a good eye for design and could imagine any of the hundreds of trees surrounding them with colorful decorations. They were shy, though, and didn't usually talk much unless someone else brought them into the conversation.

"I like that one over there," Sophia said confidently.

"Me, too! That one is perfect!" Bella shouted as she pointed in the opposite direction of the tree Sophia had chosen. They all chuckled again as one of Sophia's friends collected their money and tied the tree to the top of the van.

Before anyone could say anything else, Bella began to chant, "Cook-ie, cook-ie, cook-ie" as she looked directly at

Jake with an arched eyebrow. No matter how excited she'd been about selecting the perfect Christmas tree, nothing would make her forget the offer of a really good chocolate chip cookie.

"Okay," Jake laughed as he took her hand. "C'mon everybody, hot chocolate and cookies on me." They trundled to the small "kitchen" and ordered hot chocolate and cookies. They were homemade and donated by church members. The flavors ran the gamut from plain sugar to extravagant Christmas cookies with sweet icing piped on in artistic wonderment. In two bites, Bella had icing all over her nose and chin.

"Okay, everybody," Cassie warned them, "one cup of chocolate and two cookies. No more." She gave Miguel and Bella a stern look. "You have pageant practice this afternoon. There will be enough activity going on without adding a sugar overdose," she added under her breath.

"Pageant?" Jake asked.

"It's the Christmas pageant here at the church," Cassie explained with a smile. "All of my kids are involved."

"Jake, come to the Christmas pageant! Please!" Bella yelled as she jumped straight up and down for emphasis. "There's going to be a real baby goat!"

"It's a lamb," Cassie corrected with a laugh.

"When is the pageant?" he asked, looking directly at Cassie.

"Christmas Eve. At seven," she said.

"Sounds like fun," he smiled. They were having a silent conversation about much more than the upcoming event. They'd shared a great deal about their lives, but both of them wanted to respect their personal boundaries even as their friendship and trust grew. He was out of relationship practice, and she was still healing. Whatever happened between them was going to require respect and a lot of patience.

"Mom said it's going to be a riot," Miguel interjected.

"I'm pretty sure Mom didn't mean for you to hear that," Cassie replied with an embarrassed grin.

"And I am an angel," Bella said around the last bite of her cookie.

"An angel, a baby goat and a riot at the Christmas pageant. I'm not sure I could pass on that combination if I wanted to," he laughed.

They all said their good-byes and headed to their vehicles. The kids were singing along with carols, tossing snow at each other. For the time being, Cassie was as light-hearted as they were. It was the one week of the year when she didn't allow worries or work to interfere with their time together.

CHAPTER TEN

Cassie would say a special prayer later for the choir director and children's ministry leader. They had not only managed to wrangle children from ages three to fifteen into the same place at the same time, they also had them singing the same song, listening when they were supposed to and staying in place when the lamb came on the scene. It could only be explained as a Christmas miracle. They all hoped that the real thing went as well as the final rehearsal.

The church had offered a version of the Christmas Pageant every year since Cassie and her husband moved into the cottage. When Sophia and Lucia joined the family, they too wanted to be involved. It was a special time for all of them, and they got to see their friends, wear costumes, drink punch and play games during the rehearsals. They had a great time, and it gave their parents a few hours of free time to take care of last minute errands and catch their breath.

Cassie had a little bit of time while the kids were in rehearsal. After she dropped them off with a stern warning for Bella and Miguel, she made the most of her time. She pulled boxes out of the tiny closet she used for storage until she located those labeled "Christmas." The entire space was no bigger than a small shower stall, but she'd managed to tag all the storage boxes and stack them just so. She'd learned to make the most of every resource she had, including space. The five of them lived in less than eight hundred square feet, but they managed to be comfortable nonetheless. It was a far cry from the mansion next door where her great-aunt-in-law lived. Cassie could have tried to guilt her late husband's old aunt into letting them live with her. But given the choice between being on her own in the tiny space or under the hateful woman's watchful eye in the mansion, she'd choose tiny every time.

The year before, she'd managed to store all their decorations, including the stockings and special towels and dishes, in two big storage containers. She dragged them out of the closet and into the living room where the kids would see them as soon as they walked in. They had already unloaded the Christmas tree, set it up in a corner where it would be beautiful and out of the way, and rearranged a few pieces of furniture so they wouldn't stumble over themselves until the New Year. Everything was ready to decorate as soon as the children were home from their final rehearsal.

She also had a smaller box of craft supplies she'd been storing. She and Bella had plans to make presents after the tree was trimmed. They had a lot to do, but it would all be fun and she was looking forward to every single minute.

She checked her watch and realized she had fifteen minutes to spare. As much as she would have loved sitting in the quiet and enjoying a cup of tea, there was too much to be done. Deciding that a nice, warm stew would be wonderful for dinner, she took some meat from the freezer and quickly chopped some onions, potatoes, celery, garlic and carrots. She would defrost the meat in the microwave and start the hearty stew while the kids sorted ornaments and began decorating the tree.

By the time her children received their last minute instructions and returned their costumes, she was sitting in her van in front of the church singing along with the radio. She laughed when Lucia threw a snowball at Miguel, and he returned the favor. He was athletic and rarely missed his target. Lucia ducked just as Sophia, who'd been in front of her, turned to tell them to hurry up. She got a snowball right in the nose for her trouble, and Lucia and Miguel both bent over laughing. Bella took the opportunity when no one had her by the hand to drop to the ground and begin making a snow angel. She would be wet from head to toe and shivering by the time they got to the van so Cassie turned up the heat and continued laughing as she watched them. She was so proud of them, all of them. Her nieces were as much hers as her own two children. She loved them fiercely.

After a few minutes, she honked the horn, and they raced to the van. They piled in, talking all at once about their rehearsal and how much practice they still needed for their songs. Miguel told a silly snowman joke, and they groaned and laughed. Bella, having suddenly remembered the best thing about the pageant yelled, "And Mom, I got to pet the baby goat!"

They giggled the entire way home and then shrieked with excitement when they saw the ornaments and decorations. Before they dug into the boxes, Cassie told them all to change out of their wet clothes and hang up their coats.
It was a bittersweet time for three of the children. Lucia and Sophia missed their parents and their own holiday traditions. Miguel missed his father, and Christmas was a time of sweet memories that sometimes made it hard to fully celebrate. To help combat the melancholy, Cassie made hot chocolate for everyone and turned on a playlist she'd created of silly Christmas songs. She knew it was a feeble attempt at distraction, but she hoped it would help them get their minds off their missing family members even for a short while.

For about two hours, they laughed and decorated the tree and their house with Christmas decorations. Sophia was in charge of the mantle, and she created a bright and festive display with white candles, layers of white fabric she had saved and other glass and white decorations she borrowed from the tree. They set out pictures in Christmas frames and other holiday tchotchkes in their bedrooms and the festive towels in the bathroom. Everything they touched had a special memory or meaning attached.

Each year, Cassie encouraged the children to take responsibility for getting presents for the people on their lists. She did this for two reasons. First, out of necessity. She simply couldn't afford to buy expensive gifts for everyone. Second, she honestly believed that taking the time to think of something that would be both meaningful and created from the heart was the best kind of present to give. It was a lesson she wanted to instill in her kids. She also knew that none of them were too young to learn the value of a dollar.

A couple of weeks before Christmas, she'd taken Miguel and Bella to a store where everything cost one dollar. She gave them each a ten dollar bill and explained they could use that to buy presents or get the supplies to make presents for everyone on their list. She warned them to think about what they wanted to do and spend their money wisely. They searched and talked and planned and, after what seemed like an eternity, decided what they would do. She already had a project in mind for Bella's gifts; she only had to talk her daughter into actually doing it. Bella usually wanted to make crowns or fairy wands or sock puppets for everyone. When Cassie told her that her idea involved using glue - a new skill Bella had recently mastered in preschool - she knew her idea would work. Bella had asked almost daily if it was "time to glue the presents."

The older girls had taken the city bus and shopped on their own. They wanted to figure out their own gifts and since they had earned the money they would spend, Cassie thought it was a great idea.

Now they were down to the final days before Christmas, and everyone was still working to finish things up. Sophia, Lucia and Miguel went to their rooms to work on their presents while Cassie and Bella set up shop on the kitchen island. Cassie had gotten some red construction paper and drawn the outline of pictures. Bella, under close supervision, would glue buttons in the outline to create fun wall hangings. With her shopping money, she'd purchased picture frames to hang them all. With Christmas music playing and her mother's undivided attention and praise, she managed to focus for almost a full hour until all her gifts were finished. She was awarded for her hard work with a pre-dinner Christmas cookie which was an almost unheard of treat.

Cassie carefully hid Bella's gifts in the cabinet over the refrigerator and assured her daughter that no one would think to look there. Bella covered her mouth and giggled at having a reason to hide something. It was a game she loved but could rarely keep up. Bella's penchant for telling secrets was legendary.

Cassie took the lid off the pot of stew that had been slowly simmering for a couple of hours. She usually had plenty of help in the kitchen on long days after work, but she loved spending time there by herself, too. Even though she was serving a simple beef stew and salad, it was a warm healthy meal she was preparing. She adored the time she spent with them around the table. She'd grown up in a home where the meals were shared with her parents and her sister talking about their days and dreams, their problems and promises. She wanted to give her children that same foundation of love and support.

One by one, the smell of the hearty stew brought the other children into the kitchen. They sang Christmas carols as they set the table and dug in.

"I have an idea I want to run by you," Cassie said as they ate. "Mr. Winters is the name of the man who accused Miguel of stealing. Miguel put his spoon down and looked at her. The other stopped eating, too, so they could pay close attention to what Cassie was about to say.

"He's a mean man," Bella offered, supporting her

brother.

"I'm not so sure about that," Cassie said, patting Bella's hand.

"He said I was a thief and a liar," Miguel scowled.

"Yes, he did, and I believe he's very sorry about that. The thing is, Jake and I were talking about it and I think Mr. Winters is very lonely," Cassie tried to explain. "His job is very important to him. Jake said it's all Mr. Winters has. I think that's very sad."

"What about his children?" Bella asked innocently. She'd been surrounded by people all her life and couldn't even imagine not having brothers and sisters.

"I don't think he has any. Or a wife. Or many friends."

"That is very sad," Bella frowned.

"You do not have to do this if you don't want to," Cassie continued, "but I think it would be nice if we sent him a Christmas card."

"A Christmas card?" Miguel repeated. "I'm not going to thank him for calling me names."

"No, you're not. You don't have to thank him for anything at all. I just think it would a nice way to forgive him, that's all."

She'd thought about it a lot and this was a good teaching moment for her children. It was one thing to forgive. Acting on forgiveness gave it more meaning than simple words ever could. She believed that by doing something as easy as making and giving a Christmas card, Miguel could be free of the entire incident. She wouldn't force him but she was going to encourage him.

"Does it have to be a fancy card?" Lucia asked, already thinking of the graphics.

"Not at all. You can fold a piece of construction paper in half, write Merry Christmas and sign your name."

They all looked at Miguel. If he didn't want to do it,

they would understand. If he did, they would all be in it together.

"Okay," he said, picking up his spoon and digging in again. It was obvious from his frown that he wasn't pleased with the idea. But if his mother thought it was a good idea, he would do it to make her happy.

They talked about other things then like what their friends were doing for the holidays and the songs they were learning for the pageant. When there was a lull in the conversation, Bella announced, "You guys won't believe what I made for your Christmas presents. And I am not going to tell you where Mommy hid them."

CHAPTER ELEVEN

"Sorry we're late, Mrs. C.," Tony said as he entered Jake's grandparents' house hauling the bottom half of the huge Christmas tree they'd found.

"No worries, Tony," she ushered him in and held the door open as Jake followed with the top half. "I was getting a bit worried, though. The Christmas tree lot isn't that far from here," she smiled.

"What? How did you know we got the tree from the lot?" Jake asked as his face turned pink at being caught deceiving her.

She shooed his question and his embarrassment away with a wave of her hand. "I've known for years," she said simply. "Quite honestly, I'm fine with it. It's easier for you boys and we always have a beautiful tree. Or two."

"We'll go get the other one," Jake said, referring to the spare they'd bought. He knew she'd find a place for it, and they all knew she had plenty of decorations for two trees. Or twenty.

"The house looks great, Mrs. C," Tony said. "It's gorgeous." The Crandall house was one of the most well-known, especially at Christmas time. It was one of the homes usually featured on the annual neighborhood Holiday Home Tour. Emaline Crandall took holiday decorating seriously. From the stone walkway leading to the front door to the two-story banister and the hand-carved elves that poked out of hiding places all over the house, there was something magical and beautiful in every room. The Christmas trees were the last thing on her to-do list this year since they weren't showing the house. This year, the decorations were for her family and close friends, and they would love it.

"Are you hungry? I think Virgie just brought in some homemade cinnamon rolls," she offered.

"Who could say no to that?" Tony answered.

"You just had cookies and hot chocolate," Jake reminded him.

"Yeah, but we had to haul those Christmas trees in here and set them up since then. I've worked up an appetite," Tony replied with a scowl.

"Come on," Emaline led them into the kitchen and poured each a cup of hot coffee. Virgie, the Crandalls' long-time cook was unpacking groceries. Jake kissed her on the cheek and gave her a hand.

When they were seated at a table in the breakfast nook, Emaline asked Jake about the store, and he told her they were doing very well. So well, in fact, it looked like they would exceed the profit projections for the year.

"That's terrific, Jake."

"Thank you. It was a real team effort. In fact, I think I'm going to ask Grandfather what he thinks about giving the employees a small Christmas bonus."

"Do you think it's a good idea?" she asked him before taking a sip from her coffee cup.

"I do, yes," he answered and nodded his head affirmatively.

"Then why do you want to ask your grandfather?"

Tony, who had already finished one cinnamon roll, wanted to disappear as he reached for another. He loved Mrs. Crandall, but he was also a little scared of her. She had a way of getting quickly and directly to the heart of a matter. He knew his friend was about have a discussion for which he wasn't ready.

"Well, we don't do that every year," he answered nervously.

"I know that. We tried to do a little something extra for the employees when your grandfather had the store, but we couldn't always. But neither of us run the store anymore. It's yours, Jake. You decide."

The look she gave him dared him to question her or disagree.

They sat in silence for a moment when she changed the subject. "Tell me about the tree lot. Were they busy?"

"They were pretty steady. I thought most of the trees would be gone by now since it's just a couple of days before Christmas, but they had plenty of stock left," Jake answered. He took a sip of coffee. "I bet they will be even busier this afternoon."

"Has Jake told you about his girlfriend?" Tony asked her around a bite of his gooey pastry.

"No, he hasn't," Emaline looked at Jake with a raised eyebrow. "Girlfriend?"

"I don't have a girlfriend," he answered with a grimace. He'd kick Tony's butt for that later, he vowed to himself. "In fact, I just met Cassie a couple of days ago."

"Where did you meet her?" Emaline was thrilled even at the prospect of a woman in Jake's life. It had been far too long. Between the lingering hurt from a previous heartbreak and the time he spent at the store, Jake took little time for himself and, from what she could see, had almost no fun. A new romance was just what he needed.

"It's a long story," he answered, trying to stop the conversation in its tracks.

"I have plenty of time," she replied sweetly and sat back in her chair.

Tony added, "The restaurant doesn't open for a couple of hours, and I have a full tray of cinnamon rolls. Take your time."

Jake told her about Miguel taking the shortcut through

the store, Eugene Winters' reaction and his first meeting with Cassie. "I felt horrible, and still do, about what we almost put that boy through," he ended the short story version.

"So you simply feel bad about an awkward situation?" Emaline clarified. Jake was holding something back, she was sure of it. "There's nothing special about this woman?"

"I mean," he began, fidgeting in his chair, "she's pretty incredible. She manages to keep all these kids in line. I mean they're terrific kids. But they live in this tiny place and they are so happy all the time. I just don't know how she does it. She has a full-time, demanding job and she's raising four children all by herself." His admiration was evident as were his growing feelings. Emaline was ecstatic. Whether Jake realized it or not, he was on the precipice of something he'd avoided for a long time: love.

Emaline knew her grandson, and she knew when not to push. "Well, she sounds like a fascinating young woman."

Then she abruptly changed the subject. "So, Tony, what are your plans for the holiday?"

As his best friend regaled Jake's grandmother with stories about the restaurant and its holiday patrons, Jake thought about what she'd said to him. He certainly agreed that Cassie was fascinating. She was funny and thoughtful and smart and beautiful. He'd marveled at her relationship with her children and her sister. He and his grandparents were very close, but there were just so many people in Cassie's family. He didn't know how she managed. She had been devastated by her husband's death. That was clear. But she'd come through it and he sensed she was stronger and tougher than she'd been before. She would have to be.

He was so lost in his thoughts about her that he didn't realize that Tony was standing with his gloves in his hand and his jacket on. "Hey, Dude!" he yelled. "Don't you have a store to run or something?"

"Oh, yeah," Jake shook his head as if to clear it. "I was just thinking about the Christmas Eve rush. I'd better get back."

Emaline would have bet her life that Jake wasn't thinking about the store at all. Again, she wouldn't push. Yet.

"You'll be here for Christmas Eve dinner, right?"

"Yes, ma'am. I wouldn't miss it," he smiled as she pulled him into a tight hug.

Countdown:
2 days until Christmas

CHAPTER TWELVE

"I love oatmeal!" Bella shouted the next morning as she entered the kitchen. The girls had gotten up early and started breakfast. There were only two days left before Christmas and they wanted to do something special.

Cassie walked into the kitchen, still in her pajamas and fleece robe, slippers on her feet. She'd stayed up half the night finishing Miguel's sweater and starting on a new, last minute project. Her eyes were bleary and her hands cramped from the needle work she'd done for hours.

"Hey, girls. Thank you," she kissed them each on the top of the head.

"Good morning," they responded with a smile.

Miguel bounded into the room, already dressed and ready to go. He grabbed an apple out of the fruit bowl and headed for the front door.

"Hey, mister, hang on there. Where are you going?" Cassie stopped him in his tracks.

"The Park. Eric just called. The guys are going to meet up to sled down Hunter's Hill. Can I go?" he begged.

"Of course you can go," Cassie smiled. She was so glad he'd made good friends at school and she loved that he wanted to be outside. "But you need to eat first."

Miguel's smile turned into a resigned sigh. "Okay," he slowly walked back into the kitchen, shoulders slumped. He didn't even take off his parka or hat.

"Hey, we made oatmeal for you," Lucia frowned. "And it's delicious." She wasn't really angry. She just wanted him to understand that having to stop for a meal wasn't the worst thing that could happen to someone. Before the teasing could begin in earnest, Cassie's cell phone rang.

"Hello?" Then after a break, she said, "I'm sure she would love that. Let me check."

"Bella?" she said to the little girl who was stacking sliced apples and raisins on her plate. "Would you like to go play with Lilah for a little while?"

Bella shrieked and clapped in delight. "Li-lah! Li-lah! Li-lah!" she answered.

Cassie laughed and returned to Lilah's mother on the phone. "I believe that's a 'yes.'"

They made the arrangements for drop-off and pick-up times and Cassie urged her daughter to finish breakfast so she could bathe and get dressed for her playdate. Miguel finished two bowls in record time, thanked Lucia and his mother and ran out the door. As they finished, Sophia asked Cassie if she could drop the older girls off at Crandall's when she took Bella to Lilah's house.

"Sure," Cassie replied. "I'll be happy to drop you off. Have you decided to take Jake up on his discount offer?"

"We're not sure," Sophia answered vaguely. "We want to look around the store first. It's been a long time since we've been in there."

"Okay, well, let's get ready."

They quickly cleaned up the kitchen and were showered and dressed within the hour. They loaded into the van and Cassie made the rounds and returned home. For the second day in a row, she had time to herself in her own house during the day. It was almost unheard of in her life and she was determined to make the most of it. She brewed a cup of tea and turned on some Christmas music. She set the alarm on her cell phone just in case she lost track of time. She lit the fire and pulled her new knitting project from the drawer, took a sip of tea and immediately fell asleep.

CHAPTER THIRTEEN

Jake tried to hide his surprise when his grandmother walked through his office door. She almost never came to the store anymore.

"Hello, Grandmother, is everything okay?" he asked.

"Yes, of course it is. Can't I do a little last minute Christmas shopping at my favorite store?" She leaned over and kissed his cheek as his amused assistant offered coffee. Emaline declined explaining that she hoped to pull Jake away for lunch. The look he gave her warned that it would be a difficult task to get him to leave the store, especially so close to Christmas.

"So what's this visit really about?" he asked. He knew her better than to believe she was just out and about and wanted to have lunch. She lived her life much more purposefully than that.

She sighed heavily. Why couldn't men just learn to play along? Show a little goodwill every now and again? Why must she always get right to the point?

"I've been thinking about our conversation yesterday and a couple of things occurred to me," she began. He pushed away from his desk and sat beside her on the sofa.

"Okay," he said, giving her his full attention.

"First, about the store. I know your grandfather has told you this many times, but let me reiterate. Crandall's is your store now. The products, the look of the place and most assuredly the employees are yours. You make the decisions. And before you say anything," she continued when it looked as though he wanted to respond, "if we didn't have every confidence in you, it wouldn't be yours."

She let that sink in for a moment.

"Jake, I spent some time in the store today, and I realized that you haven't changed much since you took over. That is not what we intended. Your grandfather was ready to retire; there's no question of that. And we are both enjoying our time together. But as you will see someday, there comes a time in any business when it's time for a fresh perspective and new ideas. We want the store to grow and prosper, not remain a relic or a memorial to old times."

He wasn't sure what to say so he remained silent.

"Ever since you were a little boy, you've always been cautious. As your shop teacher in high school told us, no one ever had to tell you to measure twice and cut once. No one that I've ever met likes making mistakes or failing. But that's the best part of life! Making mistakes gives you the freedom to try again. And again. And again!" She patted his arm for emphasis. "So you try something new and if it doesn't work, change tactics, find the wind that fills the sails and move on."

"You're being very philosophical today," he grinned at her. She was giving him the freedom to handle his business and his life as he saw fit. He had pinned himself into a corner. She was showing him the way out.

"I don't mean to be philosophical. I mean to be practical," she said seriously. "It's time to step into your full potential, Jake. Be the man you already are."

"I don't want to let you or Grandfather down," he said simply.

"You can't. This business, as much as we love it, has nothing to do with how much we love you. You have brought tremendous joy into our lives. You simply cannot let us down," she smiled at him again.

"Thank you, Grandmother, I ..." he was interrupted by a knock on the door. "Excuse me, Mr. Crandall, but these ladies asked to see you."

He stood as Lucia and Sophia peeked around his secretary.

"Hey, there," he exclaimed. His day was full of surprises. "I'm happy to see you."

"Hi, Jake," Sophia said, almost shyly.

"This is perfect timing. There's someone here I'd love for you to meet. This is my grandmother, Emaline Crandall. Grandmother, these beautiful ladies are Sophia and Lucia, Cassie Shaw's nieces. I told you about them yesterday."

"Ah, yes, I remember." She stood and shook their hands. "Are you girls out doing some shopping today?"

"Yes, ma'am, we are. We were hoping to get Jake's help with something," Lucia answered.

He invited them to join Emaline and him in the seating area and offered tea or soft drinks. They declined politely, and Emaline was impressed with their demeanor and manners. They'd been taught well.

"How can I help you girls?"

"We'd like to get something for Cassie, something special. We have had such a good time this week, and we wanted to give her something to remind her of that. We thought it would be kind of funny if we bought her the necklace that man accused Miguel of stealing, but we don't know which one it is," Sophia said.

They'd talked with Miguel about it the night before. They didn't want him to be upset. His incident at Crandall's had led to them meeting Jake. They'd had a great time with him all week. They decided to give Cassie a memory of how it all started. It would be a testament to the fact that bad times can turn around and lead to wonderful opportunities.

"I see," he said with a serious face. He wasn't at all sure that was a good idea. He liked the thought and creativity behind it, but he was afraid Cassie would never have good memories associated with that particular necklace.

"I'll be happy to go down to the jewelry counter and take a look with you. I know just which necklace it was. Did Cassie tell you that I've offered a discount for your family?" he asked them.

"Yes," Lucia answered, "and we appreciate it. But we really want to pay for this ourselves."

Again, Emaline was impressed. "Before you go, tell me about your holiday plans," she invited them. For the next few minutes, they told her about the church pageant and their traditional Christmas brunch at home. They told her about Bella and Miguel, and she laughed at their stories. It was obvious that they loved their family very much. They were delightful girls. Suddenly, Emaline couldn't wait to meet Cassie and her children.

"I have an idea," she said. "Why don't you and your aunt and cousins join us for an early supper tomorrow evening, and then we will all go to the pageant together."

They were stunned. Jake had already been so nice to them. Now they were being invited to his family's house on Christmas Eve. "I don't know," Sophia hedged. "We will have to leave early to get ready for the pageant. I'm not sure how much time we will have."

"We always eat early on Christmas Eve. So many last minute details to attend to, you know." Jake looked at his grandmother in utter shock. They never ate dinner before seven o'clock, no matter what day of the year it was. "You could join us around five and have plenty of time to get to church. Then we will follow you there and watch this lovely program you're presenting. How does that sound?"

"Like the most magical Christmas ever," Lucia wanted to say. "It sounds amazing," she said instead. "We will have to ask our aunt, of course."

"Of course!" Emaline said. She pulled a small card from her purse. "Just give her this. It has our telephone number and address on it. She can call with any questions, but I will expect to see all of you at five tomorrow evening. It will be so much fun!"

She couldn't wait to go home and tell Oliver about their guests. Virgie would prepare enough food for an army anyway, but she would be surprised at their early dinner hour. Emaline was thrilled to have guests for Christmas Eve. It had been a long time since they'd shared the holiday with friends and family.

"Now, you three go ahead and find Cassie's necklace," she stood and retrieved her coat. "Make sure you get it gift-wrapped downstairs. They do a great job. Jake, will you call the car for me? I'll see you tomorrow," she said as she waltzed out the door.

Jake had always thought she looked regal. She had more style and class than anyone he'd ever met but the idea of hosting a dinner party for Cassie's family had put an extra pep in her step. All he could do was shake his head and smile.

As she requested, he made sure someone was getting her home safely. Then he escorted the girls to the jewelry department where they spent a half hour searching for the necklace. He convinced them that they had sold out of the specific necklace they'd come for and suggested a much nicer one in its place. He assured them it was the same price and winked at the sales clerk when he "confirmed" the sale price. They had no idea he was selling it to them at more than a fifty percent discount.

"Thank you for your help," Sophia said as they walked to the store's back door. "I liked your grandmother a lot, too."

"I think it's pretty clear that she likes you, too," he smiled. "I'm glad you came by today, and I'm looking forward to seeing you again tomorrow." He held the door open for them and greeted other customers who were coming in to shop. "Tell your aunt and cousins I said hello, okay?"

"Okay," they said as they walked out into the cold wind.

"Oh, I almost forgot," Sophia snapped her fingers. "Could you please give this to Mr. Winters? It's from all of us."

Jake was sure the surprise was evident on his face. "This is for Mr. Winters?"

"Yes," Lucia confirmed. "We thought he might like a handmade Christmas card."

They waved one last time as they walked out the door. Jake looked at the envelope in his hands and the elegant script that proved it was intended for his security chief. The Shaw family was teaching him a great deal about the Christmas spirit.

He watched the girls cross the street and begin the walk home. Snow was falling again but the sky was bright and sunny. It was a perfect day. Another perfect day, he corrected himself with a smile.

CHAPTER FOURTEEN

"Girls, I don't think we can do that," Cassie said after they excitedly told her about the unexpected invitation. It was obvious from their expressions that the children were disappointed. "We have the pageant tomorrow night. Remember?"

"Yes but Mrs. Crandall said they were all coming too so we would have dinner early. There will be plenty of time to eat before we have to leave. Just like if we have dinner here," Lucia pleaded.

"It's really nothing more than a change in location," Sophia argued.

"It's a lot more than that," Cassie huffed. She had everything planned down to the last detail for the next couple of days. Wars had been declared with less precision. There was still a lot to do before they celebrated Christmas. Going to dinner at the Crandalls' was going to require more preparation than just getting into the van and taking off.

She also didn't understand why the Crandalls were being so nice to her and her family. If she was honest with herself, that was really the problem. She was certain that Jake had told his grandparents about the mix-up with Miguel, and they felt bad for the boy and his mother. They may even feel sorry for her family after Jake told them about their living conditions. While she appreciated the invitation, neither she nor her children would be pitied or petted.

"You can't wear your usual Christmas Eve clothes to the Crandalls'. You'll have to wear your very best outfits. That means a tie for you, young man," she said to Miguel who, surprisingly, took the direction in stride.

"And I'll have to take a hostess gift of some kind. We cannot show up empty-handed." It was really more of a problem for Cassie, and it wasn't that hard to solve.

"I can take care of that," Sophia offered. "I have a couple of ideas that I can throw together pretty quickly and they'll be beautiful."

"And I can help," Lucia offered.

"I can help, too!" Bella yelled from the sofa. She was busy playing with her favorite dolls and had no idea what they were discussing. But if help was needed, she wanted to be in on it.

As usual, Bella's enthusiasm broke the tension. Cassie laughed. "Okay, okay," she held her hands up, "I give. We will go. But you guys," she pointed to each one of them individually, "are going to have to make sure you have absolutely everything you need for the pageant before we leave. We won't have time to run back by here before we head to the church. Understood?"

"Yes, ma'am," they all readily agreed. "Okay, I'll call Mrs. Crandall. Miguel, find your nice pants and shirt. We need to be sure they still fit, and I'm sure they could use a hot iron."

Emaline Crandall could not have been more charming when Cassie called to accept her invitation. In fact, she seemed genuinely excited about meeting them and going to the Christmas program. They chatted for a few minutes and then Cassie called Jake.

"I don't know if your grandmother knows what she's gotten herself into," Cassie remarked when he answered his cell phone.

"Cassie, I promise it was completely spur of the moment. I had no idea she was going to invite the girls or I would have called you first. I was as blindsided as you must feel," he said.

Cassie believed him. She didn't feel manipulated, just

surprised. "My whole brood is jumping on the ceiling. They are so excited," she laughed.

"I hope that means you're excited too."

She hadn't thought about it. She stopped for a second to take her emotional temperature.

"Actually, I am looking forward to it," she said honestly. She would be happy to meet Jake's grandparents - he had talked so admiringly about them - and she knew the house would be beautiful. She was also excited to spend time with Jake again.

"Good. That's good," he said.

She thought she heard him exhale as if he'd been holding his breath. He would be thrilled to see her. He'd thought about little else for the past two days.

"Well, I know how busy you must be," she said, realizing that there was no legitimate reason to keep him from the store any longer.

"There are a few things happening here," he admitted. The store would stay open late that day and then until noon on Christmas Eve. Other than the day after Thanksgiving, these would be the busiest days of the year for him.

"Okay, I'll see you tomorrow," she said.

"I can't wait," he answered. They were both smiling as they ended the call.

After he disconnected with Cassie, he decided to take another tour of the store. He'd done so several times already but he was energized by the crowds and loved to help when he was needed. Before he headed to the sales floor, he picked up the card for Eugene and walked to the security office. He had promised to deliver it personally and he was going to do just that.

He knocked on the security office door. When no one answered, he tried the handle and found it unlocked. He walked in. It had been a long time since he'd visited this office and he was chagrined at the fact that he couldn't recall the names of all his security personnel. A bank of computer monitors and workstations ringed the windowless office and he stopped at each one to look at personal photos and mementos, trying to get a better feel for the men who worked there.

He knew that Eugene's station was the one by the door. It was bigger than the others by inches and, unlike the others, held nothing of personal value. Other than a nondescript coaster and a plain white coffee mug, there were no signs that anyone sat at that station. Jake placed the card on the keyboard where it couldn't be missed. He looked around the room, wondering what it would be like to work here every day with no view to the outside world and walked out.

One more thing to add to his list.

Christmas Eve

CHAPTER FIFTEEN

Christmas Eve began a little after dawn for Cassie, and she was soon joined by Sophia. Cassie ironed Miguel's trousers and dress shirt until they were perfectly smooth. Then she went over the pants with a lint brush, just in case. She pulled out a pinafore dress with a white turtleneck shirt for Bella. The shirt was fairly new, but she'd worn the dress a year before. It still fit well enough, but it was too short. She showed it to Sophia who thought she could add a couple of rows of ruffles at the bottom that would thrill Bella and add length to the dress.

Sophia had purchased Christmas fabric that she'd fallen in love with at the fabric store months before. It was a special order piece and the factory had shipped a double order so she'd gotten the remnant for a song. Using that as the base, she designed a beautiful pillow that would work with any Christmas holiday decor. She would take it to the Crandalls' to thank them for their hospitality. She knew it was an unusual gift but she thought Emaline would appreciate it all the more because it was from the heart. Sophia and Lucia had gotten the distinct feeling that Emaline was a believer in all things Christmas.

Sophia and Cassie worked quietly in the kitchen, enjoying each other's company. By the time the others joined them, Sophia had designed the pillow, cut the fabric and trim and pinned the pieces together. All she had to do was sew it, stuff it and finish it off. Her sewing machine was in her bedroom, and she didn't want to wake the other girls so she'd waited until they were awake before she finished the gift. Then she would work on Bella's dress.

Each child would have their own work time in the kitchen. In addition to figuring out gifts for everyone, they also each decided how to wrap them. Cassie was always as excited to see their creative wrappings as she was the presents inside. After they ate breakfast, Lucia was the first with kitchen time. No one else was allowed in the kitchen when wrapping was going on. It was tradition.

After a little while, Lucia emerged from the kitchen with gifts wrapped in recycled data paper she found in the school's computer lab. She'd attached bright red bows on the green and white lined paper, and it actually looked like a traditional Christmas present. Miguel was next up for kitchen time, and he emerged with presents awkwardly wrapped in newspaper and tied with twine. From the looks of them, Cassie thought they'd need a hunting knife to get through the cord and open the present. He had made homemade gift tags from red construction paper. All of the girls complimented his artistry, and his face beamed.

Bella had chosen to spend part of her dollar store money on the gaudiest gift bags she could find. She, of course, thought the red, purple and gold velvet bags with drawstrings were the most magnificent things she'd ever seen. Cassie was certain that she would want to use them as purses when Christmas was over. She managed to put her framed wall hangings in the bags but needed help with name tags. Not surprisingly, she asked Sophia to help. They made name tags for Cassie, Sophia, Lucia and Miguel, and there was one present left.

"Bella Button, did you get yourself a present?" Sophia asked, not surprised at all. Bella loved presents and would even wrap one of her old toys to unwrap on Christmas morning. She always acted surprised when she opened it and would wrap and unwrap the same toy over and over, acting delighted every time she opened it.

"No, that's not for me," she said. "It's for Jake."

"Oh, that's very sweet," Sophia said. "Are you going to take it to him tonight?" Sophia asked as she artfully wrote his name on a card.

"No, he's going to be here in the morning."

"I don't think he is, Bella. He will be with his grandparents in the morning," Sophia didn't want her to be disappointed.

"I think he is going to be here," Bella replied seriously.

"Did you invite him?" Sophia asked. She would be very happy if Jake joined them in the morning. But she couldn't imagine that her aunt had invited him.

"No, but I know he's going to be here," Bella answered. They'd all learned not to challenge her. More times than not, she was right about this kind of thing. For a four-year-old, she was quite prescient.

Since Sophia was already in the kitchen, she wrapped her presents next. She'd taken old jeans and made unique messenger bags for everyone in the family. They were part wrapping and part present and she was glad she'd gone that route since her gifts were under the tree in less than fifteen minutes. She still had to finish working on Bella's dress for the Crandall's dinner party.

Cassie was the last to wrap presents. She'd bought a roll of beautiful wrapping paper and huge bows for the kids. They would each get three gifts from her. Cassie's sister had also sent gifts already under the tree. Bella had been looking at them longingly for a couple of days. When Cassie added her gifts, it was an amazing sight. There were gifts surrounding the tree and stacked on top of a table next to it. It was remarkable, Cassie thought, what could be given from the heart with just a little imagination.

The afternoon was a whirlwind. Sophia finished Bella's pinafore, and the little girl wanted to put it on immediately and never take it off. Everyone had to shower, which was a feat in itself since they had one bathroom. The timing had to be perfect for an adult woman, two teenage girls and two children to prepare themselves for a special dinner and the pageant. There was makeup to put on and makeup to pack. There were costumes to be checked and music to practice. The Angel kept forgetting her lines in an unexpected bout of stage fright.

Cassie scrambled to find a festive bag for Emaline's gift. She was going to stop by the store on the way to the dinner party to pick up a bottle of wine. The pillow that Sophia made was gorgeous. She'd managed to find time to weave beads into the design. It was simply beautiful, and Cassie had no idea where the girl found the time since she'd done that and everything else in less than a day. As Cassie wrapped it in tissue paper and then wrapped the box in the beautiful wrapping paper she'd used for the children's gifts, she was once again astounded at Sophia's talent.

Five minutes before they left, Cassie called them into the living room and gave them each a final once over. They looked beautiful in their finest clothes, and they were brimming with excitement. This, she thought, this is the look of Christmas. Anticipation and excitement mixed in with a lot of love.

They bundled up in their coats and loaded their bags for the pageant and the Crandalls' gift into the van before making sure they were buckled in and ready to go. As usual, their day was matching up perfectly with Cassie's schedule.

CHAPTER SIXTEEN

The Crandalls' home looked like something right out of a magazine. They walked up the flagstone walkway, lined by holiday lanterns, oohing and aahing over the red bows on every window of the Georgian style house and the red ribbon striping the columns on the front porch. They could see Christmas trees with lights twinkling and other decorations in several of the windows.

The door opened as soon as Miguel rang the bell.

"Welcome, everyone!" Emaline said as she opened the door wider for them all to enter. They stood in the foyer like the Family Von Trapp, waiting for inspection.

"Is this a mansion or a castle?" Bella asked Emaline seriously. Cassie closed her eyes in embarrassment. Miguel slapped himself on the forehead, and Sophia and Lucia just shook their heads from side to side.

"Well," Emaline said with a chuckle, bending down so she was eye to eye with Bella, "we just think of it as home. Would you like to see the Christmas decorations?"

"Who do we have here?" Oliver asked as he and Jake entered the foyer together to welcome their guests.

"We have Bella!" the little girl shouted joyously and held her arms open to Jake. He picked her up and gave her a tight hug. "Are you ready for Christmas, Princess Bella?" he asked, and she giggled and nodded her head up and down vigorously.

"So let me introduce everyone. You've met Bella," Jake said with a smile, still holding the beaming girl, "this is Miguel,

Lucia and Sophia." They each shook hands with Emaline and Oliver. "And this," he said as a smile reached his eyes, "is Cassie. Everyone, these are my grandparents, Emaline and Oliver."

Cassie handed the bottle of wine she'd bought on the way to Emaline. "Thank you so much for inviting us for dinner tonight," she said.

"You should not have gone to the trouble," Emaline said as she accepted Cassie's gift. "But I appreciate it," she winked.

Sophia handed her the wrapped box with the gift from the children. "And this is from the rest of us. Merry Christmas," she smiled. Cassie realized again that she had a very natural, confident grace about her. She was going to be a remarkable businesswoman.

"How kind of you," Emaline accepted the gift with equal grace.

"Bella," she turned to the little girl who was looking around in wonder. The staircase had been decorated with garland, and white beads and ribbon. The huge tree Jake and Tony had placed in the corner by the steps had thousands of twinkling lights and white and crystal ornaments. It was strikingly beautiful. There was so much to see everywhere they looked.

"Bella, would you like to take this gift and put it under the family tree? Jake will show you where it is. We'll unwrap it later," Emaline said.

Bella carefully took the gift and followed Jake and Oliver to the formal living room where another tree, this one decorated with old fashioned ornaments, stood in front of the windows. There was a fire crackling in the fireplace. Once again, signs of the holiday had been added everywhere from the greenery around the candles to the golden angels on the mantel.

"C'mon kids," Jake turned to them, "I have a room I

think you'll love."

"They are wonderful children," Emaline said to Cassie.

"I think so," Cassie smiled as she watched them troop after Jake.

"We have a few minutes before dinner. Why don't you and I have a glass of this wine and relax?"

"That sounds wonderful," Cassie smiled. "It's been a busy day."

"I imagine so," Emaline laughed. "You do have four children, and it is Christmas Eve."

The women walked into the living room, and Emaline found a corkscrew and two wine glasses in a discreet bar set into a built-in bookshelf. She poured a glass for Cassie and handed it to her and then poured a glass for herself.

"Very nice," she said, raising her glass. "To family at Christmas." Cassie raised her glass and they toasted with a smile.

"Jake has told me a bit about you, but I'm so glad we have a chance to chat by ourselves," Emaline said.

In fact, Jake had told her very little about Cassie. The number of times her name had come up over the past couple of days was enough, however, to let her know that Cassie was already important to him. As were the children. He was having a blast with them all and Emaline was delighted for him.

"You live close by, right?"

Cassie told her that their cottage was just a few streets over. "We're behind the house where Helen Shaw Baines lives," she finished.

"Helen Baines?" Emaline seemed aghast. "Are you related to her?"

"I was, through marriage. My husband was her great-nephew," Cassie explained.

"You poor thing," Emaline patted her hand. "Helen Baines is the meanest woman I've ever met! I'd live in the cottage behind her house too. If she had one hundred rooms in her house, no one could live with her," she finished with a long drink from her wineglass.

Cassie couldn't restrain her laughter. Finally, someone who confirmed what she'd believed since she first met the old woman. Cassie's husband hadn't known his great-aunt well when he suggested the family stay with her during his deployment. Helen considered it generous when she offered the cottage, a two-bedroom space with about eight hundred square feet, to his widow and four children. There were more bedrooms than anyone needed in Helen's house, a place she rarely lived, but where her presence was unmistakable. In fact, Cassie and her family could probably live there without Helen ever knowing it.

"Let's just say I don't use her as a role model of generosity with my children," Cassie said to Emaline.

They chatted a few more minutes and their conversation was punctuated with their own laughter as well as boisterous guffaws from another room close by. The children, Jake and Oliver were obviously having a great time together.

At exactly 5:20, Vergie appeared in the living room doorway. "Emaline, dinner is ready," she said.

"Wonderful!" Emaline exclaimed. "Vergie, this is Jake's friend Cassie. Cassie, this is Virginia, or Vergie as Jake always called her. She is the best cook in the world."

"Thank you for making Christmas Eve so special for us," Cassie said as she shook Vergie's hand in greeting.

"It was my pleasure. And hearing those children laugh really makes it feel like Christmas, doesn't it?"

As if on cue, another roar of laughter bounded down the hall. "I'd better get them."

"I've already called them," Vergie said. "If they are hungry, they'll come."

Emaline led Cassie to the dining room which, like the rest of the house, had been gorgeously decorated. There was a small tree on the side buffet, and the tablescape had fresh roses and greenery along with artfully arranged miniature Santas. Candles were lit throughout the room giving it an intimate and calming feeling. The dining room table was huge, especially to Cassie who was used to eating at a narrow kitchen island. Place cards had been set at each place.

"Mom, you should see the playroom!" Miguel nearly shouted as the children joined them.

"Yeah, Mom, you should!" Bella hopped, literally, into the room. "I played darts!"

"Darts?" Cassie and Emaline shrieked at the same time, looking directly at Jake. Neither could believe any of them would give Bella a sharp object to throw.

"Yes, darts," he replied with a smile. "Bella would guess whether we were going to hit black, red or green. She got it right almost every time. I'm thinking of taking her to Vegas," he explained.

"Yeah! I'm going to Vegas!" Bella shouted, having no idea what she was talking about.

"Did you wash your hands?" Cassie asked her.

"Yep, with Sophia," Bella said, climbing into her chair. "This is my seat 'cause the paper has a 'B' on it." She was very proud of herself.

Emaline and Oliver sat at opposite ends of the table. She could tell by the color of his cheeks and his broad smile that he was having a wonderful time with the children. She, too, was having fun getting to know them all, especially Cassie. She already understood why Jake was so enchanted with her.

On either side of Emaline were Cassie and Bella. Cassie offered to trade places with Jake, who was on Bella's right side. The little girl might need help and encouragement to try some unfamiliar foods they were eating. Emaline assured her that she and Jake could handle the situation. Jake looked hopeful but not exactly confident.

On Oliver's right was Lucia, and Sophia sat to his left. Miguel sat between his mother and Lucia and was happy he would be able to hear any part of the conversations around him. He thought Jake was really cool, and he'd never been around anyone like Oliver. Cassie noticed that he hung on every word either of them spoke.

Over roast beef, mashed potatoes, spiced Brussel sprouts, green beans and buttered corn, they all laughed and told stories and jokes. Oliver shared some stories about Jake's childhood that left him blushing and the others laughing. Lucia and Sophia told Oliver about their business ideas, and he offered encouragement and gave them thoughtful suggestions. Bella ate enough mashed potatoes to fill a small boat, and Miguel, much to Cassie's surprise, tried at least a bite of everything, including the sprouts.

It had been a perfect meal. They would have loved to linger over their apple pie longer, but they had to get to the church for the pageant. Before they left, Emaline asked if they could spare a few more minutes. When Cassie agreed, they all went back to the living room where she produced a small gift for each of them. For Lucia and Sophia, there were earrings. For Miguel, a remote-controlled car that would drive everyone crazy. Cassie received a cashmere scarf, and Bella opened a tiny necklace with an angel pendant.

"Look, it's an angel," Bella said in her high-octane voice, "just like me!" Cassie was sure she was referring to her part in the pageant. "Oh, thank you, Grandmother," she said, hugging a surprised Emaline. Everyone in the room had tears in their eyes at her innocent joy.

"Open yours," Jake suggested to Emaline as he handed her the box Sophia had given her when they arrived. Carefully, she unwrapped the gift and was thrilled with the pillow. When she was told that Sophia made it, she looked the girl square in the eye and said, "You and I are going to talk, young lady. You have remarkable talent." Sophia, clearly pleased with the compliment, hugged her as tightly as Bella had.

"Okay, gang. We have a pageant to get to!" Cassie stood and clapped her hands. They were right on time but she knew that could change any second if they didn't get going.

"Jake," Bella said, holding her arms over her head in what Jake assumed was the children's universal sign for "pick me up." He happily obliged. "You're still coming to the pageant, aren't you?"

"Are you kidding? I wouldn't miss it for the world. Is it okay if my grandparents come too?" he stage-whispered.

"Yay! Yay! Yay!" was the reply and they all laughed.

Cassie promised to save seats for everyone as they waved goodbye and clamored into her van. Within minutes, they were at the church along with fifty other children and their parents, putting on costumes and soothing last-minute nerves. Several Sunday School rooms had been taken over for final preparations. There were angels, choir singers, bell ringers, and wise men running all over the place. Mary and Joseph were present and trying to referee an argument between two angels about whose doll would portray baby Jesus. The two adults in charge of the whole thing were trying mightily not to pull their own hair out while wishing they'd had a glass of wine with Christmas Eve dinner.

Sophia and Lucia made sure everyone's costume was right. Sophia made last minute repairs to torn hems with duct tape and safety pins. Miguel and some of his friends were playing basketball with a wadded up piece of paper and a trash bin. The baby lamb had made its appearance known by immediately peeing on the carpet in the nave. It was total and complete chaos.

Cassie and the other parents and families were

mercifully unaware of the impending disasters happening backstage as they took their seats in the sanctuary. Christmas music was playing loudly, and everyone was in good spirits. She knew better than most how difficult the holidays could be.

When her husband died, nothing was joyful. Not even the holidays. She was happy now, happier than she'd been in a long time. Mostly, she knew, it was because her kids were happy and settled. It had taken time, but they'd done it. She was also ready for some new challenges in her own life. Her promotion, thinking about law school. And then, there was Jake.

The minute she thought about him, he was there. He and the Crandalls arrived just as Sophia and Lucia joined her. Cassie asked the girls how the kids were holding up backstage. All she got in response was a look of abject fear on the girls' faces.

Oliver and Emaline took their seats, and Cassie sat between Emaline and Jake. Sophia wanted to sit on the end of the row. She'd promised the choir director she would be available in case there was an emergency of some kind during the show. After what she'd seen backstage, she would bet on there being at least one.

Lucia had programmed graphics that would serve as the background for the show. At exactly seven o'clock, the sound of jingle bells could be heard over the loudspeaker, and she clicked a remote control to start the show. The first warning that this would not be the solemn event they had planned occurred even before the kids took the stage.

They had not been told that the show would start with the sound of jingle bells. So, naturally, when the loud bells started ringing, the younger children believed Santa Claus had arrived and began to cheer. It took the children's minister, the choir director and the pastor to convince them that it was just part of the show. By then, the audience had heard the commotion and had a hard time keeping their laughter to a minimum.

Fifty-three children, the vast majority of whom were under the age of twelve, took the stage in an abnormally ordered fashion. Proud parents excitedly exclaimed "there she is" or "look at him" from all around the sanctuary. Bella and her co-angels were among the first to enter and sat at the foot of the altar. She did, quite honestly, look angelic, Cassie thought. She cast a side glance at Jake and saw that he was beaming.

Miguel was among the last to enter and was a member of the choir. He had an okay singing voice, he knew. He was really there for the trash can basketball and hanging out with his friends. But he would never tell his mother that.

Astonishingly, the show was a huge success despite a few snafus. Two wise men refused to say their lines. The baby Jesus, a "real life baby doll" programmed to cry at certain times, began to wail about halfway through the program. Some children, like Bella, were intent on playing their roles and making sure their friends did the same. Bella spent as much time keeping the other angels in line as she did singing and clapping. No one in her family was the least bit surprised.

Nor were they surprised when she lost patience with the very hesitant lamb who refused to take part in the program. The plan was that after a heartfelt rendition of "Away in a Manger," one of the older children would lead the lamb through the church and everyone would follow them to the life-sized nativity outside. They would have a final prayer, and everyone would be dismissed. It was the pastor's hope that by ending the pageant outdoors, the attendees would be encouraged to leave, and he could get home early enough to put his son's bicycle together for Santa.

Despite a great deal of pleading, cajoling and even attempted bribery with a carrot, the lamb refused to do its part. After a few minutes, the lamb handler gave up and handed the rope to a choir director. She, too, tried everything she could. The children began to lose patience, and the audience's laughter went from quiet to boisterous. Suddenly, in the midst of everything, Cassie heard a single voice shout,

"Come on, baby goat, Santa's coming tonight!"

That was all it took. The audience began to laugh uproariously. The children began to shout "Ba-by goat! Ba-by goat!" The lamb's owner, afraid that the commotion and noise would cause the lamb to lose control of its bodily functions, picked it up, yelled, "Everybody follow me!" and ran outside with the lamb cradled in his arms. Instead of the one-by-one organized assembly line they had arduously practiced, the children leapt up and scrambled outside, their parents hurrying to grab their coats and follow.

Calm was restored pretty quickly once everyone was outside. It was too cold for them to dawdle. The pastor said the final prayer, including a special blessing for baby lambs and goats all over the world and dismissed the shivering throng.

"Now that's how you do a Christmas pageant!" Oliver exclaimed after the final "amen." He hadn't had this much fun in a long time. He and Emaline would laugh about it for days. They hugged the children and Cassie, wished them all a Merry Christmas and told Jake they'd wait for him in the car.

"Did I do a good job, Jake?" Bella asked, batting her eyelashes. She was certain that she'd been great, but a genuine compliment never hurt.

"You were outstanding!" he praised. "Brilliant! And your brother sang beautifully, too," he ruffled Miguel's hair. "Now, are you ready to go to bed? Christmas morning will be here before you know it!"

"Let's go, everybody," she grabbed Sophia's hand and turned toward their van.

Laughing, Cassie said, "Wait a minute, wait a minute.

Aren't you going to tell Jake Merry Christmas?"

"Isn't he coming to Christmas at our house?" Bella asked.

"Well, um..." Cassie began. They hadn't even discussed it.

Sensing her embarrassment, Jake tried to get her off the hook. "Christmas is your special day with your family, Bella. I will see you soon, though. I promise."

His response was just what Cassie needed to hear. He had never, and would never, try to invite himself in. He would wait until she was ready to include him. It took a great deal of pressure off her shoulders. Knowing that he wanted to be a part of their lives without insisting that she let him in made all the difference. They could go at a comfortable pace to get wherever it was they were going.

"Would you like to come over tomorrow?" she asked him.

"I would," he smiled. "What time do you guys get up?"

"I set my alarm for four thirty," Miguel offered helpfully. And seriously.

"I don't think I'll be there then," Jake replied just as seriously.

"Just come over when you feel like it," Cassie laughed. "We will get up early, but we won't have breakfast until nine or ten."

"Okay, I'll see you in the morning," he said. He hugged the girls and slapped a high five with Miguel.

As he drove his grandparents home, he realized that he was humming. His grandmother, sitting in the front passenger's seat, held his hand and sang along. He decided he'd stay at their house tonight. He wanted to wake up and celebrate with them in the morning. He was excited.

After all, it was the night before Christmas.

Merry Christmas

CHAPTER SEVENTEEN

By the time they got home and unpacked the van, the excitement of the day was taking its toll. They put on their pajamas and gathered in their tiny living room to eat popcorn and watch the Grinch. It was their tradition and one they loved. They had the lines memorized, even Bella, and could recite them with every character.

As the credits rolled, Bella yawned loudly. The children took to their rooms and Cassie tucked them all in, including Sophia, and whispered to each how they had made her wishes come true. That, too, was a tradition and one she treasured. She made sure to tell them every day that she loved them, but she also wanted them to know that she thought of them, each one of them, as a rare and treasured gift.

She spent a few minutes getting ready for bed and making sure everything was all set for the next morning. The last thing she did was pull a storage box out of the closet. She'd labeled it "cleaning supplies" because she knew that even if they searched diligently for their gifts, they'd never look in a box with that particular label. She had completed the camouflage by putting empty cleaning containers on the top and burying the unwrapped gifts from Santa underneath. She placed them under the tree, turned out the lights, fell asleep and dreamed of baby lambs, angels, family dinners and Jake.

At precisely four thirty-one on Christmas morning, Cassie was awakened by Miguel shouting, "He was here!" Immediately after that came the pitter-patter of little and not-so-little feet running to see what Santa delivered.

There was a new sewing machine for Sophia and a

printer for Lucia. Cassie's sister sent money and specific instructions for their gifts months before. Each of the girls also had new trousers and boots. Miguel had a new sled, a basketball, and jeans. For Bella, there was a stuffed lamb that said "Baa. Baa," when squeezed, doll clothes and a tea set.

"Momma, look," Bella cried. "Just like the pageant," she squeezed the lamb. Cassie already felt sorry for it. "I'm gonna put on my angel costume and dress up my baby and have a tea party!" she announced.

"Don't you want the rest of your gifts?" Cassie asked.

Bella threw down everything, including the lamb, and jumped up and down.

Each child handed out the presents they had wrapped, and then they took turns opening them. Bella was first, of course. They were afraid she would chew her own arm off if they made her wait in front of a pile of presents.

Cassie watched, amazed and grateful as she saw the gifts they'd given. Bella opened a beautiful dress and headband Sophia made for her. She opened her gift from Lucia and said, "Look, Mom, Lucia gave me a certificate. It says I'm the best sister of all."

"Let me see that," Sophia said with mock jealousy. She read the paper Lucia had designed for Bella and started laughing so hard she doubled over.

"What's so funny?" Miguel asked.

"Bella Button, you may be the best sister, but this isn't that kind of certificate."

"It isn't?" Bella was confused.

"Nope. It's a gift certificate. Lucia is going to teach you how to make cookies!"

"That's awesome! I'm the best sister, and I'm going to make the best cookies!" Even as she made her pronouncement, she was opening her gift from Miguel. "I love it!" she shouted and jumped up to hug him. They were very close, as close as two siblings could be, but physical affection between them was rare. Miguel had given her a coat for her doll. He'd bought it at the dollar store. To Bella, it was priceless.

She opened the presents from Cassie last. She'd given her a new doll and a new coat to replace the one she was rapidly outgrowing. She had also knitted a new pink hat and mittens to go with it. "Thank you all very much," Bella said seriously and hugged her family tightly.

Miguel was next to open his gifts. He opened a set of books and a computer game from Sophia. Lucia had saved an old laptop from the recycling center and refurbished it for him. It was an incredible gift that he treasured. Bella's button art for him was a star, and he hugged her and bragged on her artistic ability though he was sure Cassie did most of the work. From his mom, he opened a beginner's archery set, which he loved, and the sweater she'd so recently finished knitting. It was made of thick, dark blue yarn, and it would keep him warmer on his walks to and from school. The last gift he opened made him cry and hold tightly to his mother. She had taken his father's army medals and had them framed in a small shadowbox. It was a tribute to the man they both loved. She reminded Miguel as he held her and cried that his father would always be with him and would be so proud of him.

They were still crying when Bella, who had left the room to start her tea party, came back for her new doll clothes. "Hey, what happened? Did Santa leave you some gold?"

"No, goofball, Santa did not leave me any coal," Miguel answered and wiped his eyes and nose on his pajama sleeve. "Momma just gave me a gift that made me very happy."

"Let me see it," she demanded.

"It's okay," she said, clearly unimpressed and not understanding the tears, "but it's not as good as the star I made for you." With that, she retrieved her doll's clothes and went back to her tea party.

"Okay, Lucia, your turn," Cassie said, wiping her own eyes.

Lucia opened Miguel's gift first and found a painting he'd done of her parents' house in Mexico. He'd done a good job with it and was pleased that she liked it so much. She was Cassie's shy girl who kept her emotions close. Her praise for the painting meant a lot because it was obviously genuine. Sophia gave her a pair of stylish jeans and a jacket she had updated. They were perfect for a young woman who was more focused on her work than her wardrobe. Bella's button design for her was her name in a data font. Cassie's gifts were gift cards to her favorite tech store and an online class. She'd also knitted a beautiful sweater for her.

Sophia opened Bella's present first and thought it was so cute that her button art was a mitten. For Sophia, Miguel painted a cover of Vogue magazine with a black dress and Sophia's name. It was as if he was giving her a visualization of her goals and dreams. As her sister had been, she was impressed with his thoughtfulness and his talent. Cassie gave her money to use for more clothes from the vintage store, the backbone of Sophia's business. She also gave her an hour-long session with a business bookkeeper. Everyone who saw Sophia's designs, including Emaline Crandall, knew she had a bright future. Cassie wanted to make sure Sophia fully appreciated the business side of her creativity. As with the others, Cassie knitted something special for Sophia, a stylish scarf and hat. Sophia was most surprised by her sister's gift. Lucia, with a generous discount from the tech store she frequented, managed to buy Sophia a laptop that would be useful in her design work. Sophia was floored. She looked around at all she'd been given and said simply, "Best. Christmas. Ever."

Cassie had no idea what to expect from any of her children when it came to her gifts. They had been intentional in what they gave each other and seemed to have chosen perfect gifts for everyone. She meant what she'd whispered to them the night before: they were her true gifts. And they were perfect for her.

She smiled as she looked at Sophia and reached for her gift first. "I love the wrapping," she remarked. "This bag will come in very handy."

"Yeah, Sophia, I meant to say that, too. I'm going to use mine as a book bag for school," Miguel added.

"I'm glad you like it," the older girl responded to both.

"I want one of those," Bella said with a frown as she made yet another trip through the living room.

"You have one, silly," Sophia said.

"Uh, uh," she insisted, "I didn't get one."

Miguel held up her bag on one finger and spun it around. "So I guess this one's mine, too, huh?"

"Hey, give me that," Bella lunged for it.

"So much for Christmas spirit," Cassie said. "Are we already having an attitude, Bella? It hasn't been that long since Santa left."

"I'm sorry," the youngster answered with pouting lips. "I'm just tired."

They all laughed out loud. Bella was no more tired than the man in the moon. It was something she'd heard other people say to excuse their bad behavior. She knew full well they always laughed when she said it.

She smiled, feeling certain that all was forgiven and went back to the girls' room to play.

Cassie looked inside the messenger bag and found a gorgeous dress Sophia made for her. "Oh, Soph," she cried. "This is amazing." She stood and held it up to herself as if modeling it. The color and cut were perfect for her. "I love it," she said as she hugged her oldest niece.

She sat and looked for the gift from Lucia. "It's an

envelope like Bella's. Am I the best aunt in the world?" she teased, referring to Bella's interpretation of her certificate.

"Well, yes you are. But that's not what the certificate says," Lucia laughed.

Inside was a wonderfully designed coupon book with twelve coupons for homemade dinner. "Can I cash these in for the next twelve days?" Cassie asked Lucia seriously.

"They're yours," the girl responded, clearly hoping that was not really Cassie's plan.

"You know I love your cooking and this is going to be so helpful throughout the year," Cassie said. "Thank you so much." It was a gift from the girl's heart. She was an excellent cook, but she didn't love spending time in the kitchen. Unlike Cassie, Lucia didn't escape through cooking. She always pitched in to help, they all did, but this was an offer to take control and provide meals for the whole family.

Miguel handed her the gift from him. He'd done a painting for her, too. This one was of the scales of justice, and she wondered how much he knew about her hopes. He would be an important part of her future plans. They all would. She realized she needed to talk with them about what she hoped to do. It was important that they know she still had dreams and was willing to chase them.

She also had a surprise gift from Bella, a button wall hanging like the others. Her design was a snowflake. She called her youngest into the room. "Am I in trouble?" Bella asked as soon as she walked in. "Of course not. I want to know how you snuck around and made this without me. We did not make this together during our work time." She held up the snowflake to show her.

"Do you like it?" Bella asked, snuggling up beside her mother.

"I do not like it," Cassie said seriously. Seeing the look on Bella's face, she quickly added, "I LOVE it!" She grabbed her daughter and hugged her until Bella giggled and said, "I can't breave."

"How did you do this?" she asked.

"Sophie and Luce helped me. Lucia held the flashlight, and Sophie helped me glue," she whispered conspiratorially.

"You made this in the dark?" Cassie asked, looking from one girl to the next.

Lucia shrugged. "It was the only way you'd be surprised."

"Well, I sure am," Cassie said. "You tricked me!" Those words were like music to Bella's ears. Nothing made her happier than tricking people.

"I believe this has been the best Christmas ever," Cassie announced.

"Should I make a certificate for that?" Lucia teased, and they all laughed.

"How about we clean up some of this mess and then start breakfast?"

As soon as the words were out of her mouth, there was a knock on the door.

"Yay, Jake!" Bella shouted as she jumped out of her mother's arms and ran for the door.

"Merry Christmas!" he shouted, his arms full of gifts.

Cassie hoped she would have time to change out of her pajamas and robe before he arrived but such was life on Christmas morning at the Shaw household. They greeted each other with a smile as the kids circled him and told them, all at once, about their gifts. It was then that Cassie noticed more gifts had appeared under the tree.

"Come in," Bella said. "We have presents for you!"

"Presents for me?" Jake asked. He was surprised and flattered. "Well, I have a few things here, too."

"Presents for me?" Bella echoed him.

"Come in, sit down," Cassie invited him. The fire

burned brightly and candles were lit throughout the room. Christmas carols played and the room had the general ambiance of a happy Christmas. Except for the four children and the volume, it reminded him of the first time he and Cassie sat and talked for hours. Could that have been just a couple of nights before?

He and Cassie sat on the couch with Bella so close, she was practically in his lap. Sophia had the only other chair in the room. Lucia and Miguel shared an ottoman. If Norman Rockwell had painted the twenty-first century family, they might have been the model. Bella handed him a package wrapped in the most garish velvet bag he'd ever seen.

"Open mine first," she chanted. "Open mine first!"

He pulled the button angel wall hanging from the bag and looked at it in awe. "Did you make this?" he asked Bella, holding it like it was a priceless painting.

"Yes," she answered shyly.

"It's beautiful. Shall I hang it in my office or my apartment?" he asked her. It was definitely going on a wall where he would see it often. She shrugged her shoulders in confusion.

"I think you should hang it where it will bring you the most joy," Cassie offered.

He nodded in agreement. "You're absolutely right. Thank you, beautiful Bella. I love it."

"I love you," she shouted and threw her arms around his neck. He was stunned at the completely spontaneous declaration.

"I love you, too," he said, looking over her head at Cassie.

"Open mine next," Miguel offered, handing him a small package wrapped in newspaper. Jake opened it to find a deck of playing cards. "You know, I used to love to play cards," he said. "I just haven't had anyone to play with in a long time."

"You could teach me," Miguel offered. Jake's reaction was exactly what he'd hoped for.

"That would be great," Jake smiled and offered a high five.

Cassie smiled. Jake may not have spent a lot of time around children, but he was a natural. He encouraged and supported without ever patronizing them.

"Let's see what I have here," Jake said as he reached behind him for the presents he'd brought. "This one is for Miguel and this one is for the princess Bella." he handed the boxes to them.

Bella ripped into hers like a madwoman. She opened the plain box and then stopped all action as she drew in a deep breath. "It's beautiful," she whispered. She opened the top of a jewel encrusted box and a tiny ballerina, in a pink tutu and toe shoes, popped up and twirled while music played.

"I knew Grandmother was getting your angel necklace," he explained. "I thought you might like to have a jewelry box to keep it in."

"Oh, I love it!" she said, still in awe as she watched the ballerina turn. She showed it to each of the girls expecting, and getting, the appropriate amount of ooohs and ahhhs.

"Are you kidding me?" Miguel suddenly screamed. "No way, no way, no way," he was shaking his head from side to side in disbelief. "No way, man."

He looked at Jake who answered, "Way."

"What do you have, son?" Cassie asked. She couldn't imagine what he'd received that caused such an uproar.

"Jake gave me tickets to a football game. A real football game. The pros," Miguel explained. He'd never been and barely dared to dream of going. This was too much.

"That's very generous," Cassie looked at Jake, pointedly.

"Company seats," he mouthed as if that explained it all

away.

"Mom, is it okay if I ask Jake to go with me?" Miguel asked.

"Of course. I think that would be most appropriate, in fact," she smiled. He was so excited.

"Jake?" the boy asked, unconsciously holding his breath as he waited for a reply.

"Already on my calendar," Jake laughed. This time there was no high-five. He wrapped Jake in a hug almost as tight as the one Bella had laid on him. Jake patted him on the back as he returned the hug. Cassie could tell this was a very emotional experience for him. It was for her, too.

"This is from Sophia and me," Lucia handed him a box wrapped in data paper. He didn't have to wonder who was in charge of wrapping.

He opened the small box and found a business card holder made of supple black leather. It appeared to be hand-stitched.

"We didn't think the one you have is really....you," Sophia explained. They'd seen the gold metal version on his desk. She had found this one at a vintage clothing store she frequented and couldn't believe it was in such good shape.

"Thank you, girls," Jake said, touched that they had noticed this tiniest of details. "You're right, of course. I had never thought of it." He opened and closed it over and over and finally put it in his pocket.

"My gift for the two of you is really a gift for me," he told them. "I would like to offer each of you a job at Crandall's." They looked from him to one another and back to him again.

"Doing what exactly?" Cassie asked.

"Well, I'd like for Sophia to be a style consultant for our young women's brand. And I'd like to invest in her business by carrying her designs when she's ready for that," he began.

Sophia sat with her mouth hanging open. It was the kind of thing that only happened in books and movies. "My grandmother was so impressed with your style and the work you did on the costumes and the pillow you made. And my grandfather was equally impressed with your business acumen. They both told me that if I missed this opportunity, they wouldn't," he said.

"I can't believe it," she said.

"You should. This is just the beginning," he smiled. "And you," he turned to Lucia. "I need your help immediately."

"I can't sew," she said and everyone laughed.

"I know very, very little about computers, but even I know we are way behind the times. We need to update our technology. I have no idea where to begin. I need you to work with our new Director of Technology on what young people expect. You guys shop differently than our older customers do. I'm finally ready to make some changes in the store, and this is something that needs to be addressed sooner rather than later. You up for the challenge?"

Lucia looked at Cassie for permission. This would be a huge responsibility but it was an opportunity she wanted to take.

"As long as school is still your priority," Cassie said but they both knew that Lucia didn't need the reminder.

"Of course, for both of you," Jake readily agreed.

"I'd like to give it a try," Lucia said.

"Great. I'm excited for both of you. But I'm more excited for me. And relieved," he smiled.

"I have one last gift," Jake said and wriggled his eyebrows at Cassie.

"Me, too," she smiled.

"Wait a minute before you open Jake's gift, Mom," Miguel said.

"Why? What's wrong?"

"Nothing is wrong. We have one more gift for you to open first."

"Another gift for me?" she asked, surprised. "You guys have already been so generous."

"This one is from all of us," Sophia said.

"Yep, all of us," Lucia smiled as she took the box from her sister and handed it Miguel.

"Mainly it's from me," Miguel said with a wry smile.

"No, it's not. It's from me, too, Mom," Bella announced. "And Jake."

"And Jake, too? Well, now I am intrigued," Cassie said with a smile. "Should I shake it?" She held it close to her ear.

"No, no, no," they all said in unison.

"Okay, no shaking," she answered, surprised at their response.

"Okay, I'm going to open it but first would someone get the last gift under the tree and give it to Jake?"

"Yeah," Jake agreed, rubbing his hands together vigorously. "Let's get that last present over here."

Bella giggled as she handed it to him.

"Okay, go!" she said.

They opened the lids at the same time and both drew in a breath.

"This is beautiful," Cassie said as she pulled the gold multi-pronged starburst on the thin gold strand out of the box. "Someone help me put it on," she said. Sophia rushed to help. They'd be waiting all day if Bella tried to work the tiny clasp.

"This is gorgeous," she said again, "but you spent way too much money on this."

"We wanted to get it for you because it's kinda like the one Mr. Winters said I stole," Miguel said.

"But it turned out great 'cause now we have Jake!" Bella said. "Hey, I made a rhyme. Turned out great 'cause we have Jake, turned out great 'cause we have Jake," she began to singsong.

Cassie blushed at the silly song. She didn't know if they "had" Jake. He'd been very nice to her and wonderful to the kids but it was Christmas. Who knew what tomorrow would bring?

"Cassie, I don't know what to say. This is amazing," he said, breaking into her thoughts. He'd opened the scarf she knitted for him. It was dark gray and black with specs of tan throughout. It would match his warm coat perfectly. He put it around his neck and smiled. "It even smells good," he said, recognizing the special scent she wore. It was her one personal indulgence, and he'd noticed it almost immediately when they met.

"I'm glad you like it," she was pleased. She'd only finished it the day before and had worked almost around the clock, catching ten minutes here and there when she could find it.

"Okay, last one," he said, handing her the last small box. She opened it and found an exquisite gold bracelet with an intricate clasp. It matched the starburst necklace perfectly.

"Oh, it's beautiful," she exclaimed. It was much more extravagant than the scarf she'd given him. It was too much, in fact.

Before giving her a chance to object, he reached for the clasp to show her how it worked. "I thought it would be nice to have something that goes with the necklace. You know," he held her hand and looked directly in her eyes, "like a set."

She knew he was going to kiss her. It had been a long time since she'd received a Christmas kiss from a man she cared for. When their lips met, there was a chorus of "yeahs" from her children.

Bella put one of her tiny arms around Cassie's neck and the other around Jake's. "My Christmas wish came true," she said dramatically.

"Mine, too," said Miguel.

"Ours, too," said Lucia and Sophia together.

Cassie and Jake laughed, embarrassed that their feelings had been the subject of so many wishes. Then they shrugged and admitted the truth to each other and the children.

"Ours too."

Author's Notes

Christmas is always a special time for me because I have a wonderful family and family of friends. My ability to write stories and my life in general wouldn't be possible without their support and love.

Special thanks to my first reader for this and every other project from my term papers to my books. My Mom was always the first to read and tell me how brilliant I am (whether it's true at the moment or not). My Dad doesn't have to read a word I write and still supports every idea, no matter how crazy, that finds its way to my laptop.

Dora McCary and Becky Johns are "my girls" and gave me tremendous encouragement and thoughtful comments on the first draft. This journey wouldn't be nearly as much fun without them. Thanks girls!

My BFF, Shannon Rizzo, always props me up (sometimes literally) when I'm ready to finish a project and there is still much typing to be done. She has read my drafts on airplanes all across the world. She also loves baby goats – so I found a way to give her one through Isabella. Thank you, Shannon, for all of it.

My editor, Jacque Hillman of the HillHelen Group, gave me edits and comments that made this book better and will help my writing as I try to tell better stories. She did so this time on an unbelievably short deadline. Jacque, I appreciate your support, encouragement, insight and friendship more than you know. Thank you for being a part of this.

Finally, all my love to Jackson, who makes my world brighter and lighter every single day.

Thank you for purchasing this book!

I'd love to connect with you and give you a few freebies that I've created just for my readers!

You can find me here:

www.jenniferrawls.com
Just stop in and say "hello"
Sign up for my monthly newsletter
Find out what I'm writing next
Grab a little something free from me

FACEBOOK
Join my group of Strong Women (and men)!
Take part in the discussions
Be a part of the community

PINTEREST
Check out what inspires me to write upcoming books
Share what's important to you
Get some inspiration to be the Strong Woman you are!

INSTAGRAM
Get inspired
Share a laugh
Let's learn more about each other!

Made in United States
Orlando, FL
08 May 2024